NIGHT SWEATS

A NOVEL

BEAU SAVAGE

To my mom,
resident hot flash expert,
and my number-one fan for life.

NIGHT SWEATS

PROLOGUE

SHE HANGS BY HER WRISTS, choked together with frayed rope that bites into her skin as she teeters and sways in the dark. Too weak to stand, suspended too high to kneel, she simply dangles there, all her tired weight pulling on those ropes, on her wrists, knotted to the metal hook fastened into the basement's exposed ceiling.

She's been hanging for days now.

Her naked body is a tapestry of fine crimson cuts. A gruesome work of art, as well as a great deal of meticulous torture. She can hardly see it for herself, can hardly marvel at what she's become, what's she's been *made into,* but she feels every wound like a burning script across her body. If she could see it, or run her fingers across the raised edges, she's sure the script would read:

I'll be dead soon.

She knows she's not the first. She also knows she won't be the last.

The ceiling above her head groans. Footsteps pound the

floorboards. Dust settles down through the moonlight coming through the window at her back, casts her sorry shadow upon the concrete before her. She can barely hold her eyes open, but she rolls them slickly heavenward to the sound of his footsteps. Pounding. Pacing. She traces him across the ceiling, toward the door at the top of the basement stairway which she can't see but knows is there just around the corner.

The door opens. Those heavy footsteps creak the wooden planks, scuff the cold cement. The artist appears from around the corner. He comes to stand before her, gripping his instrument in his fist—sharp and twinkling.

"Tonight's your lucky night," he says.

He's come to finish another masterpiece.

PART ONE
NIGHT SWEATS

ONE

BARBARA

THE ONLY THING worse than crying in a public restroom is being caught crying in one.

I'm standing at the long bathroom counter, leaning against it with both my hands braced against its lip, my head hanging low because I'd like to avoid seeing myself in the mirror like this. Not just struggling to hold back my tears, but... *like this*, like I *am*.

Old.

I'm getting older every day. I know that's true for everyone. I know it's an unavoidable fact of life. Time passes, you age. I'm *aging*. It happens so gradually you hardly notice it at first, for a while, until suddenly the universe cruelly forces some ill-timed frame of reference in front of you to demonstrate *what was* and *what is*, how old you've become. Usually it's a photograph from years prior that catches you off guard, or the inability to complete some physical task you used to be able to perform with ease.

For me, it's the eyes. I hardly recognize mine anymore.

They're as blue as they've ever been, except now I find them smack dab in the middle of WWI trench warfare. *Crow's feet,* as some like to call them. I'm being dramatic, I know. To be completely honest, I'm skirting the actual issue here, anyway. It isn't simply due to age that my eyes have changed. There's so much more to it than that. Circumstances play a large role, too. More than I'd like to admit right now, as my vision blurs and trembles with emotions I can't hold back any longer.

Even in the midst of this, I can't help but remind myself that I'm too old to be crying in bathrooms.

The bathroom door swings open. A shrill whine. There's a bit of a walk from the bathroom door to the bathroom itself—a kind of blind hallway buffer before turning the corner—which allows me to escape into the nearest stall and shut the door before anyone can see me losing my marbles in plain sight. Still, the haste with which I slam the door and loudly slide the lock likely informs whoever it is of my deliberate escape—that I'm avoiding them.

I take a seat on the toilet. My nose is running and I have to sniff a little to stop from making a mess of myself. The newcomer's footsteps traipse daintily into the stall next to mine. The door shuts. I see the hem of a dress for a moment before she pulls it up and takes a seat herself. That simple glimpse of her dress is enough for me to immediately identify who it is.

Oddly, I relax a little.

It's not my boss. Nor is it anyone from marketing, whom I can't really stand, to be truthful. It's just Cassidy, the bringer of office treats. Obviously that's not her real job.

She's a technical writer like me. But she's notorious for bringing snacks into the office, oftentimes delicious, home-made pastries and baked goods. I struggle to recall a single morning I've greeted her that she *hasn't* warned me about some temptation she's left in the break room. She's always a friendly face, though, and probably the least concerning of anyone who might catch me crying like I am.

In my relief, I let out a shuddery breath that immediately betrays me—an exhalation thick with all the emotion I was trying to conceal.

"Barbara?"

Cassidy's voice floats to me from beneath the stall, somehow both echoey and muffled at the same time.

"Yes?" I reply. My voice comes out a bit *wet,* so I clear my throat. Another giveaway.

"Is everything all right?"

Well, no, everything is *not* all right. But I can't help thinking this is an inappropriate time to be having such a conversation, sitting beside one another in bathroom stalls. Granted, I'm only faking it. Probably she knows that. Either way, she isn't shy in the least bit as she relieves herself even in the midst of asking the question. I'm almost amused enough to smile, but not quite.

"I'm fine," I lie.

Before Cassidy has a chance to ask anything further, I stand up and flush the toilet. I hurry out of the stall and return to the bathroom counter where I started. I catch a glimpse of myself along the way. I *look* miserable. Like I haven't slept in days, which I haven't. I crank the faucet on, rinse my hands a bit, crank it off, and tear a paper towel from the dispenser just as the toilet flushes from Cassidy's stall. I crumple the paper towel up and toss it into the garbage before my hands are even completely dry. But I'm still not fast enough. Cassidy emerges from her stall—big bright blonde hair, sparkling brown eyes, and a surprised sort of smile that's perpetually glued to her face, like she's in constant awe of the world around her. I notice the flicker of pity in those brown eyes, however, as she sees me, as if my visible misery has startled her.

"Hold on a second," she says, stopping me in my tracks as she begins washing her hands at the sink. She makes eye contact with me through the mirror as she bends down with her hands in the water. "How would you feel about grabbing lunch?"

"Today?" I say, and immediately wince for having said it. Of course that's when she meant. When else?

I scramble for some excuse. I find one, an obvious one, and feel it inching toward the tip of my tongue when Cassidy beats me to the punch.

"Yeah, there's this really cute sandwich shop that just opened across the street. I've been there once already, and they have *the best* paninis. Seriously."

"I don't know," I say, that excuse of mine still locked and loaded. "I've been kinda feeling a little—"

"You're not fine." Cassidy looks fully over her shoulder at me as she says it, leveling her eyes on me with a certain, deliberate honesty about her—a gentle way of telling me she knows I'm full of shit. "I can tell."

I don't know what to say to this. My mind blanks. Not many people would be so bold, to call me out on my avoidant, suffer-in-solitude behavior. Because I know most people don't actually care. I'm surprised Cassidy of all people would be so bold.

She turns off the water, shakes her hands a couple times into the sink, and begins drying them with a paper towel as she looks at me again in that knowing way.

"Join me for lunch," she says, "and tell me all about it."

TWO

BARBARA

IT'S CROWDED inside the sandwich shop, so we opt for the outdoor patio instead, despite the middle-of-August Tennessee heat. It's shaded at least. We pick a table away from the doors, where the inside chatter is farthest but the nearby traffic is closest. I don't mind either way. Cassidy sits perpendicular to me at our little round table. She smiles as she pulls her chair in, then clasps her hands under her chin, elbows on the edge of the table.

"So," she says, and lets out a big breath. "How's this?"

"It's great," I say, and force a smile.

Honestly I'm not sure how to feel about any of it. About her. I hate to keep harping on the age thing, but I'm considerably older than Cassidy. Not old enough to be her mother, by any means, but our ages are just far enough apart to place us into different generational brackets, and I can't help feeling like I'm being babied by a *baby*. She smiles at me and blinks with those dark doe eyes. I pull at the neckline of my blouse repeatedly, billowing it, as if I can air out the sweat and natural humidity that's been clinging to me since our first steps out of the office.

"I know," Cassidy says. "It's hot as hell out here. But I figure this is better than shouting at each other inside."

"It's great, really."

I reach for our little plastic order-number stand on the table and turn it slightly, to ensure they find us when they bring out our sandwiches.

"So," Cassidy says again. "Should we just get right into it? What had you so worked up earlier?"

Cutting right to the chase. I simultaneously like it and hate it. I loathe small talk in most settings. I also loathe the thought of telling Cassidy much about my personal life. I can't imagine why she'd take such an interest in my well-being in this way. I hardly consider the lives of my coworkers, even on a good day.

"You know," she says suddenly, before I even have a chance to answer, "I just realized, I know almost nothing about you. We've worked together for... *two years* now?"

I shrug. "I don't think anyone around the office would describe me as being especially personable," I answer. And that's the truth. Any faults I might have, I do pride myself on being aware of them, at the very least.

"True," Cassidy says without pause. "I think I've actually heard it said a few times, *'she's very professional.'*"

Maybe it shouldn't, but this *does* make me smile. "Really? Is that what they say about me?"

Cassidy nods. "You've got this *mysterious, no nonsense*

thing going on, for sure. I think some people around the office might even find you a little scary."

"Scary?"

"Or maybe *intimidating* is the better word."

"Intimidating…"

"Actually, I'm lying. I *know* people around the office find you intimidating. Because I've heard them say just that."

I'm surprised to hear any of this. Mostly I keep to myself, get my work done, and go home. And once I'm out those doors, I hardly think about the place until I arrive again the next morning. But, of course, that might be because I don't have the luxury of fretting over office politics most days, when my mind is already burdened with plenty of other painful things…

"Naturally I was a little surprised to find you in the bathroom like I did," Cassidy goes on. "I may or may not have thought to myself *'wow, so she is human, after all."*

Cassidy smirks in the kindest way she can muster, to assure me these comments are all in good fun.

"I just…" I hesitate. I'm not even sure what I'm about to say. Part of me still can't believe I agreed to this. I don't really want anyone in the office to know my personal business. I have no interest in making friends at work. Not that I have any friends outside of work, either. "I think I'm just a bit overwhelmed, is all."

"What are you overwhelmed with?" she asks, politely prodding.

"Well…" I hesitate again. I'm not sure I should be telling anyone this yet, when I haven't even made up my mind about it. "Candace offered me the position this morning."

What I mean by *'the position'* is the soon-to-be-vacant senior supervisor position that will be opening up by the end of the month, when our current supervisor, Dustin, will be transitioning departments to fill another vacancy. I don't need to specify any of this to Cassidy, though, as this has been the topic of much gossip around the office for the better part of August—gossip I'm only privy to on account of my peers being so indiscreet.

"You mean..." Cassidy bows her head toward me conspiratorially. "You were offered Dustin's job?"

"Yes," I answer simply.

"But then you had to have applied for it, right? Did you apply for the position?"

"I did," I admit. "Though, I'm not entirely sure why at this point."

That's not true. I know why. I applied for the job because some part of me is in desperate need of a change. Some part of me needs to be *stirred.* It's like I can feel myself inside—my body and mind alike—growing as thick and stagnant as my life has become on the *outside.* My head is a hot, windowless room with no air conditioning, not even a ceiling fan, and I've become *more than accustomed* to suffering silently inside its decay.

The problem is that my awareness of this fact comes and goes in waves. At one *particular* time, it had seemed like a good idea, applying for a job promotion. A good *change.* But now that I'd interviewed for it, and been offered the job, that wave had since receded back down the shore, leaving me dry and panting and unsure why I'd ever bothered.

"Don't you want it?" Cassidy asks next.

"I thought I did." I take a deep breath. Saying it out loud somehow makes it easier. Hearing my own voice, my own words, suddenly helps to put things into perspective again. "I *do* want it. Actually, I think I *need* it. It's just, you know, other stuff comes up and suddenly everything feels like it's too much."

"What other stuff?" Cassidy gazes at me openly, her lips slightly parted and ready to inhale any morsel of personal drama she can glean. I'm beginning to get the feeling that her interest in my problems might simply be a distraction from her own, whatever those may be.

Here comes the longest hesitation of them all. This is the *real* problem. The *real* obstacle. My eyes become hot coals at just the mere notion of telling someone else. I should really be speaking to a therapist, and not just a friendly face with no credentials.

"It's the third anniversary of my daughter's passing." There. It's out in the open. My heart is slamming in my chest. "You assume it's going to get easier with time, but something about this year… three years later… it's like it's all just happened again."

The open-mouthed expression on Cassidy's face visibly pales in color at hearing this information.

"I didn't…" Now *she* hesitates. "I didn't even know you had a daughter. I'm so sorry."

I'm surprised she never heard anything around the office, at the very least.

"Well, like I said, it was three years ago," I say. "We weren't working together at the time."

"I'm so sorry." Cassidy reaches for me, places a hand on my arm. Her touch almost *hurts,* even though she's barely touching me. "That's... well, I can't even imagine."

My eyes are burning with emotion. Someone passes us on the sidewalk and vaguely reminds me we're in public. Incredibly, it doesn't stop me from continuing, like the flood gates have been opened and now there's no shutting them.

"I think my husband and I are on the brink of divorce." I can't believe I just blurted it out, but there it is. There's a good chance all this information will be spread around the office by the end of the day, or by the end of the week at the minimum. I'm in such disbelief that I'm even sharing this, that all I can do is laugh. A choked, teary-eyed laugh. "Sorry..."

"Don't be sorry," Cassidy says. "That is *so much* to deal with. I really can't even imagine. You do a great job putting on a brave face, I guess. I never would have known you were going through anything like this."

A brave face. I've convinced myself over the years that it's easier to wear one, but at this moment, sitting outside this little sandwich shop with tears springing from my eyes, it suddenly wallops me—just how exhausting it's been to keep up appearances like I have, to keep everyone *out* and *away.*

"I want the job, I do, but with everything else in my life, it just feels like more than I can handle right now..."

"It sounds to me like you need a *break,*" Cassidy says. "You know, like an honest-to-God *vacation.* When's the last time you took time off?"

I have to think about it, and the answer makes me laugh again. I swab tears out of my eyes.

"I don't even remember. Definitely not since my daughter..."

I don't finish saying it. I'm so close to squashing the emotions down again, to getting myself under control, I don't want to dig deeper. Someone will be bringing out our food any second now and I'd like to be composed by the time they do. I swallow the lump in my throat. I chance a glance at Cassidy who's looking at me now with this tilted, curious, pitying expression I hate. I think I hate it mostly because I feel like she's overdoing it. Laying it on thick. Seeing that look on her face helps to pull myself together even quicker.

"Some time away would do you good, I think," Cassidy says. "Probably a *lot* of good. Come back refreshed, clear-eyed, ready to take on something new."

I take a deep breath, fully collecting myself again. I look around just to make sure we're still the only ones seated on the outdoor patio.

"Maybe," I say.

I'm eager for our food now. Not because I'm especially hungry, but because I'm eager to have this lunch over with.

"And I don't know exactly what you and your husband are dealing with—and it's none of my business, I know— but maybe some time apart would help out your marriage, too. Take some time for yourself, you know?"

My walls are up again, and I find myself tuning her out slightly. I hear her words, I understand them, but my brain has taken over its autopilot defenses. I'm in survival mode now. Survive this conversation, tolerate it, and make a clean escape.

"Yeah, maybe," I answer.

"You know…" Cassidy pauses. It's a deliberate pause, enticing me to look at her again in anticipation. She only continues once she's got my attention. "I might know just the thing." She nods now, agreeing with herself. "Yeah. Actually, it might be perfect for you."

I grimace. "What's that?"

"Well, I've got this little vacation house. It's… well, it's my family's vacation house, really, but I swear I'm the only one who ever uses it. It's this gorgeous little thing by the lake." Her eyes move over my face, so eager to save me, so eager to see some glimmer of *hope* in my eyes. "It's where I like to go sometimes to *'get away from it all.'* Even I need that a couple times a year. It's quiet… it's *private…* with a beautiful view of the water, and the trees."

I hate to admit it, but the more she describes it, the more I find myself intrigued. I haven't even thought about taking time off in literal years. It truly hasn't occurred to me that I might do such a thing, like the word *vacation* fell out of my vocabulary, sounding foreign on Cassidy's tongue.

"That sounds nice," I say, and I'm surprised to mean it.

"I'd be more than happy to let you borrow the place for a few days, if you wanted. I think it'd be good for you."

Good for me. That's a strange thought. I haven't entertained thoughts like these in some time. Time away from home? Time away from work? Time away from my husband?

"That's so generous," I say.

"Think about it," Cassidy says.

She opens her mouth to say something else, but suddenly our food is here, our plates served onto the table before each of us.

I couldn't be happier for the interruption.

THREE

KYLIE

Kylie Grenko is a seventeen-year old hurricane.

At least she moves through her bedroom like one, tearing shirts from their hangers and ripping pants and sweaters from her dresser drawers, stuffing them into her backpack until its zipper can hardly shut without its stitches popping. She stuffs a large tote bag just the same with anything she can't bear to leave without, because she's not sure when she'll ever be coming back.

If she ever comes back.

Knuckles rap against the other side of her bedroom door. Her father's muffled voice barks through, ordering her to let him in. The door's not even locked. It doesn't have a lock, actually. Kylie could never be trusted with one. That's why she's dragged the smaller of two dressers against the door to hold it shut, to keep *him* out.

"Open this goddamn door this instant!" he bellows.

Kylie tunes him out as she snatches her favorite pair of sneakers and stuffs them into her tote bag with all the rest.

She's currently wearing a pair of running shoes, the ugly kind that are all sorts of random colors—blue, green, and yellow, these ones—with thick rubber soles she's still somehow managed to wear down to nothing. The top of her left shoe has a hole worn through the very tip where her big toe peeks through. She wears them for work—*wore* them for work?—a job which does not—*did* not?—involve running but rather a lot of walking and standing. She supposes she's running now, though, isn't she?

"*Kylie!*" her father shouts.

She's got her backpack and her tote bag each filled to their brims. She slings her swollen backpack onto her shoulder. She sets the tote bag on the floor beneath the window, drags the window open, carefully extracts the flimsy screen, and proceeds to climb out with her heavy load into the deep night full of crickets and other insect noise. She doesn't bother closing the window behind her.

She's never coming back, she decides.

She skirts the side of the house. The street ahead is deathly still, deserted, the other homes dark and sleeping like hers should be at this hour. She doesn't own a car, so she heads for the sidewalk. She's nearly there when the front door yanks open behind her and her father's enormous body hurtles through like the boulder from Indiana Jones, rumbling across the patchy lawn and onto the sidewalk at her heels, his feet scuffing madly, puffing dragon's breath from his mouth *and* nostrils. She doesn't look back. Not for a second. Not until he grabs her by the arm in front of the neighbor's house and roughly spins her around to face him. She cobra-strikes toward him, chin jutting, venom gushing from around her teeth.

"Let go of me," she demands.

He only grips her tighter. "And where *the hell* do you think you're goin'?"

Her father's formless face ripples with anger as he speaks.

"Let go of me or I'll scream."

Kylie means it. Her father knows she means it. She's always been *'belligerent'* and *'disrespectful'* in his eyes, as if his treatment of her has ever earned him more than that.

"I got a call from your boss earlier," he says, still holding tight to her bicep. "What's this I hear about you walking out on your job?"

Kylie tugs her arm in her father's grasp, uninterested in answering his pointless questions.

"I said let go. Before I wake the neighbors."

He narrows his eyes. He presses his lips together firmly —what little lips he has—so that his mouth forms a narrow black line of disappointment across his face. Then he scoffs.

"You're a spoiled little bitch, you know that?"

Finally he releases her, shoving her a little as he does because nothing can ever be gentle with him. With *either* of them, really. Kylie isn't even sure she knows the meaning of the word. *Gentle.*

"Good luck wherever you're goin' I guess," he says, and shakes his head in disbelief as he turns around and stomps his way back to the house.

Kylie remains standing in front of the neighbor's, however. For a moment or two. She watches her father cross the yard again and disappear into the dark, hears the quiet sound of the front door shutting for good. She's not sure why she's still just standing in place like she is. Had she hoped for him to turn around? At least once? Or did she watch him go because part of her is afraid she'll never see him again?

Yeah right, she thinks defiantly.

She turns on her heel and starts walking.

———

She has no real idea where she's going.

She holds out hope that she might stay with her sister in Nashville, but fears in the back of her mind that her sister will want nothing to do with her. Except that can't possibly be true, she thinks. Her sister will understand better than anyone. She did almost exactly this some five or six years ago. She and their father are no longer even on speaking terms. Kylie prays that when she shows up on her sister's doorstep, she'll wrap her in her arms and say *"Finally."*

She considers calling her sister, telling her what's happened, asking if she can stay, asking for a ride. But there *is* a possibility she'll be rejected, however slim, which terrifies Kylie more than anything. Whereas if she just shows up unannounced, although her sister might be incredibly annoyed, there's no chance in hell she'll turn Kylie away then. Not immediately, at least.

She only needs to get there first. Without a car, it'll be a while. She can't even take the bus. Not at this late hour. She can't afford an Uber, either. She thinks maybe she should have been a bit smarter, should have waited until tomorrow morning. Except then she would've had to endure her father's judgement in the meantime, the thought of which makes her blood boil.

Her father doesn't actually care that she's quit her job. He hadn't cared when she'd gotten the job in the first place—a measly cashier position at the local theater. Her father doesn't really care at all about what she does, one way or the other. Not really. He only pretends if it means he has an excuse to be angry, or an excuse to *punch down.*

In fact, her father cares so little that he hasn't asked to see a report card since Kylie was thirteen years old. He takes no interest whatsoever in her schooling, her grades, her *future.* But God forbid he receives one phone call about her skipping class. Then suddenly he cares *a lot.* Suddenly what she does *matters.*

Kylie growls with these thoughts as she crosses the street, angry that she's even still thinking about him. She *can't wait* to put him behind her forever. She reminds herself that she's already done it. He's *behind* her. She doesn't need to waste another second of her life dwelling over that old screaming fart.

Yet she can't help it.

She switches her tote bag from one arm to the other, back and forth as either of her shoulders grow tired and sore.

She leaves the quiet of the suburb and soon finds herself moseying into town. The lights of the gas station attract her like a moth. She does have some money in her pocket.

Enough for a snack and a drink. And maybe once she's there—

Kylie comes to a lopsided halt as a police cruiser pulls into the gas station parking lot. Her shoulder sings with the weight of her tote bag. She absentmindedly shifts her bag around again while she watches the officer climb out and head into the convenience store. She can't go in there now. Not yet, anyway. The last thing she needs are the cops breathing down her neck, asking why she's out so late, alone, carrying all her pathetic life on her back like she is.

She veers elsewhere. Down the next street. Away from the gas station lights, the street lights, all of it. She hobbles along muttering under her breath all the while like a sick person.

"Stupid... so stupid..."

Out of nowhere—not really—her eyes swell with tears. She blinks them back, or tries to. The street ahead swims, porch lights splintering into sparklers. Lugging her heavy load, she bumps into the chainlink fence beside her—dirty white plastic slats slotted through to provide the most minimal privacy to the yards beyond—and drops her tote bag onto the ground, where it rolls onto its side and spills half its contents onto the cement. Kylie groans. She crouches and begins stuffing her clothes and sneakers back into her bag. Her vision blurs with even more tears. Before she knows it, she's full on sobbing over her wrinkled clothes. She can hardly hold herself up, crouching like she is. She finally topples, rolling onto her hip on the cement. She catches herself, spilled awkwardly beside her spilled tote bag, and decides to stay there a moment. She scoots herself against the fence, pulls her knees in, buries her face down against them.

Maybe by the time she's done crying, the officer will have left the gas station and she can buy herself something to eat. And after that, she can... what? Start walking again? Sleep under a bridge?

Stupid. So, so stupid...

Kylie's heart shoots into her throat as a pair of head-lights sweep across her, as a car turns onto the street where she's resting. She looks up, her head springing off her knees, terrified that it's the officer driving by, by pure happenstance catching her despite her efforts to avoid him.

The car slows to a stop right beside her and she sees it's not the police cruiser at all. Someone else. A car she doesn't recognize. The window hums as it rolls down, revealing only darkness within, along with the vague shape of the driver.

From that darkness emerges a voice Kylie doesn't recognize any better than the car.

It asks: *"Are you all right?"*

FOUR

BARBARA

My DAUGHTER's honey-colored hair is styled in beautiful, bouncy curls. She's wearing a lovely blue dress—a deep blue that would greatly complement her eyes if only they were open. Her hands are clasped across her belly. Her normally suntanned skin looks paler than I've ever seen it, but I have to admit they've done a great job with her make-up otherwise, exceedingly well done considering the bruising she'd been marred with following the accident.

She almost looks alive.

I'm standing at her open casket with a line of people waiting behind me. They can wait until the sun goes down and comes back up for all I care. None of them would dare hurry a grieving mother. I clasp the edges of the casket and bawl my eyes out while my husband stands with me, an arm around my shoulder. He's bawling his eyes out, too, but he's quieter about it. Because he thinks he needs to be. For me. For himself.

I hate the thought of this being my last memory of her,

dead in a silk-lined box. And yet I can't possibly tear myself away, can't possibly turn my back on her now, even if she's not really here to see me do it. There's a part of me that fears I'll forget her face if I do. Of course it's not true. But the fear remains.

And then my daughter's eyes spring open.

Mine widen similarly. My tears immediately abate. I'm not imagining it. Her eyes are actually open. Those deep blue irises roll toward me, snap onto me with terrifying speed and precision. I feel my husband's grip tighten on my shoulder as he sees it, too. The impossible.

"She has your eyes," he says.

My entire body is tense, overcome with the urge to *bolt*, but I can't move. In fact, I'm still clinging to her casket, my nails digging painfully into the wood. My daughter just looks at me, eyeing me from the corners of her eyes without turning her head an inch. I lose my breath, can *feel* myself holding it in.

"She's always had your eyes," my husband says.

———

My eyes snap open again. For real, this time.

I awaken to the sound of my own voice rasping in the back of my throat, a slight gasp. Then silence. I'm met with only the darkness of our bedroom ceiling. I'm hot and *drenched* under the covers. I pull them gently off my body, so as not to wake my husband who appears to be soundly sleeping beside me, and expose my damp skin to the air-conditioned room. I prickle with goosebumps from head to toe, even as my body still seems to flush with heat, my face especially. Am I sweating because it's hot? Am I sweating from the nightmare? Or is this just another average night with perimenopause?

It's not the first time I've had this particular nightmare, though I haven't had this one in months. I assume I'm having it again due to the timing—the anniversary. Along with other stressors, I'm sure.

I take a deep breath as my body cools down, as the sweat dries off my body. I turn my head on my pillow to see my husband beside me. *Hank.* Sweet, handsome Hank. He's utterly silent as he sleeps, never snored a single night during our marriage, so it's hard to tell sometimes if he's actually asleep or not.

My throat is painfully dry, as it seems I've pushed all the moisture in my body out through my pores. I climb out of bed and wander discreetly into the hallway, into the kitchen, where I take a glass from the cabinet and fill it from the refrigerator fountain. I take a couple gulps from the glass to wet my palate and throat, fill it up again, and then head to the rear sliding door. I stand at the door looking out for a moment. Then I peer toward the hallway, toward our bedroom, considering. I already know I won't sleep the rest of the night.

I unlock the sliding door, drag it open, and step out into the cool dark night. The patio creaks under my bare feet as I walk to the railing and peer into the lush woods at the border of our backyard, lively with insect noise and a cool, summer night breeze. Just below the patio is an empty above-ground pool, which hasn't been filled with anything besides rainwater in over a year.

I take a couple more gulps from my glass and proceed to stare into that dark, stagnant hole of a pool. My nightmare tries to claw its way up from that hole, but I force it aside, force it *down,* and choose to remember something else in its place. Something better.

I remember her laughter. I remember so many hot afternoons spent in that pool, and her laughter as we swam and played together for hours just to escape the sweltering heat when our old air-conditioning unit went kaput.

As I stare into the shadows of the empty pool, I see flashing lights. They're not really there, they don't really exist, but I see them anyway. I always see them, even three years later. It's another memory. I'm helpless to stop this one. It barges its way in at the worst times—though I suppose there's never a *good* time, for memories like this. Flashing lights, spinning, blue and red, blue and red.

Standing at the porch railing, I close my eyes against the vision as if that'll stop it. Instead I simply provide it a better backdrop. I see the officer's face, illuminated in our front porch lights, and I can tell exactly what he's about to say just by the sorry look in his eyes. Even after all these years, my heart cinches tight as I anticipate his words, words I've repeated to myself too many times.

Ma'am, there's been an accident.

Without even realizing it, my free hand has found its way to the railing and I'm gripping it tight, which of course spurs my nightmare back into the forefront of my mind—gripping the edge of my daughter's casket, her eyes blue and *wet* with life as she stares back into mine, as her pale skin illuminates with the strobing blue and red of police lights.

I nearly jump out of my skin, nearly drop my water glass as the patio creaks behind me. A moment later, someone slides their hands around my waist. My initial surprise melts away in an instant. Hank's stubbly face brushes against my ear. He breathes slowly, and it's only a matter of seconds before my pulse slows as well, and my breathing slows to match his. His breath tickles my ear. He says nothing, just holds me from behind at the porch railing, and suddenly I just can't keep it in anymore.

I set my glass down on the railing, turn around in his arms, and press myself against him, lean into him, *claw* at him with my hands on his shoulders, and before I know it there are warm tears streaming down my cheeks and soaking into his thin shirt where I bury my face against him. He pulls me in tighter, envelops me with his strong arms. Too often I forget how strong those arms are. How secure I feel inside them.

FIVE

KYLIE

THE FIRST THING Kylie feels when she wakes is the cold cement against her temple where her head lies. A numbness there. She blinks and sees the dark. At first, anyway. As her foggy mind catches up, and her wandering eyes grow clearer, she finally feels the rope biting into her wrists behind her back. Thin, rough twine.

Cold clarity rushes through her. She spasms, jerking in place, and discovers her ankles are bound likewise. She lifts her head off the cement momentarily and winces at the kink in her tilted neck.

The basement is mostly dark. Cramped. Across from her is a wooden-plank stairway. The door at the top of the stairs is shut. The body at the bottom of the stairs is utterly still.

A body.

Kylie tenses, but not before shuddering violently from head to toe. A young woman's body lies at the foot of the basement stairs. She's completely naked, and at first glance Kylie mistakes the intricate markings on her body for tattoos. But they're not tattoos. There's visible *depth* to them. They're not just markings, but *openings.* Wounds. Cuts.

Kylie can't take a full breath. She shivers again. She writhes within her restraints. She tries to pull her wrists apart, to somehow stretch the unyielding twine. She curls her fingers and scrabbles for the knots but they're tied so tightly there's no picking or pulling at them.

I shouldn't have gotten in that car. Why did I get inside that car?

Hopeless despair floods her. She wishes she'd gone to the gas station after all. She wishes she hadn't run away from home in the first place. What was she thinking? She feels stupid for putting herself in such a vulnerable position, but of course she couldn't have known. *I couldn't have known.* All she knows, right now, is that this must be a nightmare.

This can't be happening.

The ceiling thumps with footsteps. She freezes, holds her breath. The butchered woman at the foot of the stairs holds her breath as well, but she's been holding hers since Kylie first opened her eyes.

This cannot be happening.

The footsteps pound around in circles as someone paces about upstairs, creaking and groaning, pausing on occasion. Kylie resumes her fruitless struggle to get at her restraints. There's no hope there. Another wave of despair crashes over her. She wants to cry but can't. It's only a feeling.

The footsteps finally travel to the door at the top of the stairs. The door opens. A dark figure stands in the open doorway. Wide in the shoulders. Masculine. The figure steps down onto the first stair, then onto the second, then onto the third where it stops with both feet planted firmly. It's definitely a man, Kylie can tell. He bows his shadowy head, gazing upon her. His face is masked with darkness.

A tiny voice in Kylie's head urges her to beg for release. For mercy. Then her eyes flicker to the body at the foot of the stairs and she knows there's no use in such pleading. She's never leaving this place. The dead woman there is a vision of the future. *Her* future. Inescapable. Inevitable.

Without a word, the man turns and starts back up the basement stairs, closes the door, and leaves her.

Kylie still wishes to cry, but is too terrified to shed a single tear.

SIX

BARBARA

AFTER HANK CAME and found me on the back patio, we both returned to bed and I tried to get some more sleep before my alarm four hours later. Unfortunately, I found sleep as impossible as I suspected it would be.

Now I'm stuck in rush-hour traffic, stealing glances at myself in the mirror as I brake behind the lines of cars in front of me, stealing glances at the bags under my eyes and wishing I could just call in sick and spend the whole day in bed. It's Thursday, so the weekend is still far enough away to feel unbearably out of reach.

I remember Cassidy's offer. A free stay at her family's lake house. A peaceful weekend all to myself, to spend however I please, surrounded by nature. As I inch my car forward, and listen to the sounds of my brakes squealing as I come to yet another stop, the temptation of her offer overwhelms me. A relaxing getaway sounds divine right now. Time alone, with no pressure to please anyone but myself. I haven't had that in so long. Not without feeling guilty for not making better use of my time, anyway.

I look into the rearview mirror again, at those eyes I hardly recognize.

You deserve a break. You deserve a vacation.

Those *eyes* deserve a vacation, I think. I imagine myself sprawled out on a lake dock with a book in my hands, with a cool breeze sweeping the lake and the trees around me, maybe a cozy stockpile of chocolate at my disposal while I lose myself in the comfort of solitude.

Traffic ahead is beginning to speed up again. I see cars several places ahead of my own take off, separating, scattering as they make it beyond the slowdown, whatever it is. I inch forward. I stop. I inch forward. I stop.

Then, coming around the bend I see the cause of the slowdown for myself. My heart clenches coldly in my chest.

Twisted metal. Glittering glass across the pavement. An ambulance and paramedics.

My masochistic mind takes me to obvious places. Obligatory memories, at this point. I do my best to stare straight ahead, instead of allowing myself to rubberneck like everyone else. I inch forward. I stop. I inch forward. I stop.

Finally I reach the officers directing the merging traffic, waving us through to the open lanes beyond.

I leave the violence behind me with a knot of grief in my throat.

"So, about that offer…"

I'm standing at Cassidy's desk as she's mid-sip with her morning coffee to her lips. She turns to me with wide eyes, and then smiles as she realizes it's me.

"Barbara! Good morning."

"Morning," I say. I smile in kind. I clasp my hands nervously, feeling a little strange as I address my coworker, when usually I do everything in my power to avoid idle chatter. Though, I suppose there's nothing idle about this conversation I'm initiating. "Sorry, I didn't mean to inter-rupt you…"

"Oh, are you kidding me?" she says. She laughs. "I only just got here. I'll be checking pointless emails for the next hour, at least. What's up?"

I clear my throat. "I just wanted to ask if that offer was still good."

Cassidy tilts her head slightly, as if trying to remember.

"About your family's lake house."

"Oh!" She closes her eyes for a moment, embarrassed that it took her this long to understand what I was saying. "Of course. Right. Yes! Yes, of course the offer's still good. You thought about it, then?"

I nod politely. I won't mention my nightmare, or the abysmal sleep I got last night, or the terrible accident I witnessed this morning that pushed me over the edge, transforming my interest in a relaxing getaway into a desperate *need*.

"I did. And I decided it sounds too good to pass up."

"Oh, yay!" Cassidy sets her coffee mug down on her desk, then claps her hands with a jovial smile from ear to ear. It's so sugary sweet, I almost regret everything. "I'm so glad. I think you'll love it. How soon were you thinking?"

"Well… how soon do you think it'll be available?"

Cassidy smirks. "I mean… I'm the only person in my family who uses the place. It's pretty much *always* available."

"So, this weekend?" I ask, taking my shot.

Without another word, Cassidy swivels in her chair, reaches under her desk, and pulls her purse into her lap. She digs around inside until she extracts her keys. I stand in silent shock that it's happening so quickly, with so few questions as she slides a single key off her keychain and hands it to me.

"Oh," I say, slightly dumbfounded. "Is that…"

"This is the key to the lake house," she says. She seems to notice the bewilderment on my face. "Don't worry, I've got a spare at home."

I take the key from Cassidy—just an average, silver key in the palm of my hand.

"Thanks. Sorry, I'm just…" I can't help laughing in my disbelief. "I guess I'm surprised you're so trusting, is all. To just loan me the key to your lake house, no questions asked…"

"Oh, no, I've seen the desk you keep. I know you'll take good care of the place."

All at once, the kindness of it all hits me like a truck— leaves me swerving as I try to stop myself from falling to pieces in front of her all over again. Or maybe it's just the menopause again. Lately, just about anything can get me feeling sentimental. A week ago, it was a television ad for some newfangled allergy medication that almost had me sobbing.

"I'll email you the address and some simple instructions on finding it," she says, doing me the favor of pretending she can't see the tears in my eyes. "Once you get to the lake, it can get a little confusing, with all the random turnoffs and private property signs. Anyway, I was just there a couple weeks ago, so I already know it's ready. To be honest... I think I take better care of that place than my own home."

I clutch the key in my fist. "Thank you."

"Yeah, of course! Also, I brought muffins this morning. There should still be some left in the break room. You should take one before they're gone!"

SEVEN

BARBARA

WITH THE KEY to Cassidy's lake house in my possession, and free reign to use it anytime this weekend, I find it impossible to wait. I ask my boss for time off—tomorrow, Friday. It's short notice, I know, but it's also been so long since I've asked for any time off, my boss is pleasantly eager for me to even be asking.

Now I'm at home packing. My medium-sized luggage bag is open on our bed as I stuff it with three days' worth of clothes, along with some other necessities like a couple books and my eReader for good measure. Through our bedroom window, the evening light turns gray-blue as the setting sun falls farther below the horizon into night.

It's only as I'm zipping up my luggage bag that I hear the door to the garage open and close as my husband finally arrives home from work. A late day. I've already texted him about my little lone excursion I've planned. I felt a bit guilty initially, planning something only for myself, leaving my husband home alone when he's gone just as long as I have without a vacation. But to his credit, he replied to my texts with enthusiasm, feigned or not.

I lift my sealed luggage bag off the bed just as he comes through the door. His eyes flicker between the bag and myself, and he smiles as warmly as he can.

"Are you leaving tonight? I thought you were going first thing in the morning."

"I am. In the morning, I mean. I just thought I'd pack ahead of time."

His smile broadens, becoming something real rather than just a gesture.

"You make sure to pack enough books?"

"Plenty," I say, and return his smile with a genuine one of my own.

He nods approvingly. "Good."

We stand looking at one another for a moment, my luggage bag's handle gripped in my hand as it rests on the floor beside me. Then the moment stretches into something painful. It's difficult to understand why I feel it at first, the ache in my chest. Then, as I stare into Hank's eyes, it dawns on me—the subtext.

"Am I losing you?" Hank asks suddenly, and the blunt *honesty* of the question breaks my heart into countless pieces. I release the handle of my luggage and I go to him immediately. I can't resist him. I put my arms around his neck and hold him against myself, feel his arms wrap around me likewise.

"No," I say. "No, you're not losing me. Not at all."

"I'm sorry for how things have been lately." His voice is soft and soothing and yet still full of longing and hurt that I can hardly stand to hear. "I know I've been distant. And I know…"

"You're no guiltier of that than I am," I say. I cup the back of his stubbly head in my hand.

"I know I've been prioritizing work a lot this past year… or these last couple of years…"

"We both have," I say, trying to reassure him. And it's true. I think he and I are both entirely aware of what our marriage has become, and yet we've both been so complacent, so complicit in its deterioration. I can't help but laugh a little at the idea that he thinks he's the only one guilty of this. "Anything you could possibly apologize for, so could I."

He sighs, and I feel him turn to butter in my hands, like all his pent-up guilt is evaporating off his shoulders. He really thinks it's all been on him. It's probable, I realize, that my texts regarding my little solo vacation broke him out of his own fog, made him realize how much we've both just been *coasting* all this time. Nothing's been the same since our daughter's passing, that's for sure. We've each independently allowed ourselves to settle into this monotonous groove of routine and solitary suffering.

"I don't want to lose you," he says, his words breathy and brimming with heartfelt concern.

"You're not," I repeat. "I just need some time away, is all. Some time to myself. From work and… everything." I'm tempted to suggest that maybe some time apart would do him some good, too, but I refrain. I won't speak for him or his feelings. Also it feels a bit strange to suggest I need time alone, when we've spent so much of the last three years being alone. Alone, but *together*.

His laughter relieves me.

"Maybe I'll have myself a lazy weekend, too, while you're away," he says.

"You should. Order yourself some pizza, have a few beers, and just... *pig out,* if you want."

He laughs again. I squeeze him even tighter around the neck and he reciprocates, bear hugging me. I smile a bit... until I open my eyes and my vision laser focuses on one of the framed photographs hanging on our bedroom wall. A family portrait, the three of us together: Hank, myself, and our daughter.

All at once I find myself increasingly eager to escape this house—and all the guiltier for feeling this way.

EIGHT

KYLIE

AFTER THE MAN'S DEPARTURE, Kylie waits for what feels like days but is more likely just hours. *Just* hours. It's been many hours, enough to watch as the pale moonlight on the concrete across the basement stretches, shrinks, and then shifts to early morning sunlight.

In the meantime, Kylie manages to sit herself up against the wall at her back. She continues picking at the knots that tie her wrists together behind her to no avail. She even tries getting her hands out from under her butt, thinking things would be easier if she had them out in front, but she can't manage it. She swears she saw someone do it in a movie once, but it's much harder than it looks. Or maybe she's just not quite skinny enough for it.

She thinks about standing up, thinks about hopping around the room in search of something that might help her, but by the time she starts thinking of these things the morning has already arrived and she fears the man's return at any moment. She fears being found someplace else,

having moved herself out of her little corner of the basement in search of an escape. She'll be punished for such
transgressions, she thinks. Not to mention, if there was any
hope of finding means of escape, surely she wouldn't have
been left alone like this in the first place. No, she's been left
alone all these hours precisely *because* her captor knows
there's nothing she can do, nowhere she can go.

Kylie wonders if the dead woman at the bottom of the
stairs wondered all these things, too.

She's still lying there. Unmoving. *Obviously.* Kylie
wonders how long she's been here. How long ago did she
go missing? How did it happen for her? Was she picked up
off the side of the road? Was she too trusting? When she
woke here, did she wriggle about the floor, try to slip her
hands out from behind her back and fail like Kylie did? Did
she scream for help, as if someone outside this place would
hear her? As if someone might rescue her?

How long had she been here before the cutting started?

Up above, a door slams shut. The heavy footsteps
return. The ceiling creaks and groans and sheds dust into
the morning light as Kylie lies petrified, holding her breath
as she follows his noises around the house, until finally his
movements bring him once again to the basement door. It
opens. The upstairs is much brighter than the downstairs.
The warm light spills down the wooden stairway. His
shadow stands at the top for a moment, looking down at
the body, perhaps looking at Kylie, too. It's hard to tell. He's
carrying something under his arm. A big roll of plastic
material. It crinkles against him as he starts down. At the
bottom of the stairs, he stands still, gazing at Kylie without

any doubt in her mind. For a moment she worries he'll be upset that she's moved *at all* since he last saw her, sitting up against the wall now like she is. But he says nothing.

He drops the plastic roll onto the ground beside the woman's body. It's roughly the length she is. He rolls it out flat, away from her body, toward Kylie. Then, with the toe of his boot he nudges the woman's body onto the rolled-out tarp. He crouches next to her, clasps the edge of the tarp against her arm, and rolls her over again, this time rolling the tarp with her along the way. He rolls her once more. Kylie can't see the woman any longer, except for the blonde hair that spills out from the end of the tarp. Over and over again he rolls her body, coming closer to Kylie against the wall until finally he reaches the tarp's edge. Kylie presses herself against the cement wall, away from the rolled up corpse and the featureless man standing over it. The woman's fine blonde hair is nearly touching Kylie's feet so she pulls them in, knees bent and tucked against herself.

The man places a boot on top of his plastic-wrapped victim, and studies Kylie for a long, silent while.

"Don't get lonely down here when she's gone," he says.

It's the first time he's spoken to Kylie. She hates his voice. No, she *loathes* his voice. She loathes just how *ordinary* it is. Not unique in the slightest. He could be anyone. Not only that, but he sounds *friendly*, in fact. He sounds nothing like the monster he must be. The sound of his voice sends all the wrong signals to Kylie's brain: like there's some chance he'll let her go if she just asks nicely enough, or if she does everything he says, and is the most obedient little victim he's ever abducted, maybe she won't end up just another body in a tarp.

She puts all of these thoughts out of her mind as quickly as they come, identifying them for what they are: desperation.

The man crouches down again, carefully hoists the rolled-up woman over his shoulder, and proceeds to haul her up the stairs and out of sight.

NINE

BARBARA

I'VE READ through Cassidy's instructions a handful of times, and plugged the address into my GPS app, and still I have trouble finding the turnoff. I come to a complete stop on the narrow, shaded dirt road. In just the last half-mile I've already passed several paths, many of them guarded with "PRIVATE PROPERTY" gates like Cassidy mentioned.

Unfortunately, GPS stopped being useful as soon as I left the main road. Now I'm relying on my memory of Cassidy's instructions. Just to be sure, I grab my phone and pull up my email. I'm still getting the tiniest sliver of reception up here. I skim Cassidy's instructions again, confirming that the turnoff I want is on the righthand side of the road. She also mentions that the turnoff is marked with a red signpost. I hunch toward the windshield, scouring the trees for such a marker. No such luck. Yet.

Onto the next.

I pass another turnoff on the left. Then I come to another righthand turn where I immediately notice a red-painted post at the entrance. There are no letters or messages of any kind written on the post to indicate where it leads. Still, it's a red post sticking out of the ground. I'm fairly certain this has to be it.

"Finally," I mutter under my breath.

This road is even narrower than the one before it, and bumpy as hell. It seems to curve in on itself as I follow, careful not to slide my car against any of the underbrush that tightly chokes the path on either side. Then it curves outward again, and I roll bumpily down a slight slope. Through the trees ahead, I glimpse it. A flash of sunlight off the water. A bit farther and the path spills me into a clearing, and suddenly the lake house is *right there*, nestled against the trees that grow right up against its backside. It's a decent size, with a second story where a balcony overlooks the small clearing toward the lake. My eyes are immediately drawn to that balcony—a great place to potentially read a book. There's also what looks to be a covered side patio. Again, another good place to relax with a book in my lap.

The clearing itself leads directly to the water, a short distance from the house where a small wooden dock reaches over its shore into the sunlight. There's a thick tree right beside the dock, with a tire swing fastened to its fattest branch, turning gently back and forth in a breeze.

It's all so instantly picturesque that I can't help but murmur from behind the wheel, *"Wow."*

I pull up near the front porch and park my car. I shut off the engine. I climb out, my feet crunching the dirt, and for a moment I just stand behind my open door and marvel, both at the house before me and the nearby lake softly lapping at the dock, its surface disturbed by the same breeze that turns the tire swing. Is it getting windier, I wonder? There's a constant insect hum in the trees—the cicadas, the same as in town, or anywhere else for that matter. Somehow their noise feels different here. It's peaceful, rather than merely droning.

"Wow," I say again.

I grab some of my things from the backseat and begin carrying them to the house. The porch steps squeal with each step. With my luggage bag in one hand, I navigate my keys in the other, sticking Cassidy's lake house key into the front door. It unlocks with a satisfying click. I push the door open and step inside.

I want to say *'wow'* again but I resist the urge.

Cassidy's done a marvelous job with this place. It's as cozy as cozy can be. The house's layout is mostly open, the kitchen along the far wall, with comfortable living room furniture in between, as well as a quaint little staircase that leads to an open loft upstairs—again, another perfect place to read a book.

I take my luggage to the only bedroom, downstairs to the left of the door. I dump my bag at the foot of the queen-sized bed. Then I pull the covers aside and check the bedsheets, confirming as best I can that they're clean. I'm shocked to find they still smell freshly of laundry detergent.

I fetch the grocery bags remaining in the backseat of my car and carry them into the kitchen. Cassidy mentioned this place was all on the grid, and I confirm as much when I open the refrigerator and the light comes on and I feel its

cold air against my face. The refrigerator is empty, save for
a big pack of bottled water. I put away the food I've
brought with me, leaving the dry snacks out on the
countertop.

As soon as that's done, I make my way upstairs to the
loft. There's a futon here, as well as a small TV and a bookshelf full of board games, I suppose for friendly gatherings.
I open the window behind the futon to let some fresh air in,
the upstairs noticeably stuffier than the downstairs. Then I
open another window on the other side of the loft beside
the balcony door. A warm breeze sweeps through, along
with all the insect noise.

I return downstairs to the bedroom and unpack the
books I brought, already eager to settle in and start reading.
Then again, I wonder if I should explore a little more first—
at least *pretend* that I'm here to enjoy the outdoors and the
scenery, and not just to have a quiet place alone to read.

I check my phone for any calls or texts from Hank...
even though it's only been mere minutes since I arrived and
last looked at the damn thing. Predictably, understandably,
there's nothing.

I replay last night in my head, the moment he and I
shared together.

Am I losing you?

Even now his words hurt me a little. Am I losing *him?*
Are we losing each other? Obviously asking ourselves such
questions has to be a sign that things are *not good,* but the
sincerity of the question must also mean that it's not too
late to turn things around, right?

Holding my phone in my hands, I'm suddenly hit with

a blushing heat. I can *feel* my face turn red hot, my skin prickling with sweat. I take a deep breath, a deep sigh, and set my phone down on the nightstand beside the bed. I fan myself with both hands which barely helps.

Damn hot flashes.

Wishing to distract myself, I head back outside onto the front porch. It's hot out here, too, of course. The warm Tennessee air is thick with moisture, even with a breeze moving over the lake. From the porch I can see the water, as well as the little dock that sits over it, half shaded by the surrounding trees. I make my way there. I walk halfway across the dock, standing just under the cover of shade, and listen to the water rippling underneath my feet. The lake itself is rather modest, oddly shaped as it seems to curve out of sight to the right. It glimmers with blinding sunlight. Over the trees on the other side I spot a mass of clouds rolling across the sky, moving quickly with the wind that does indeed seem to be picking up. Is there a storm coming, I wonder? I checked the forecast and saw only *'partly cloudy'* with no mention of precipitation or strong winds, but then again it wouldn't be the first time the weather surprised me.

Besides, I think maybe I'd enjoy a little storm to read by.

Standing in the breezy shade, I notice something else across the lake. Not *over* the trees, but under them. Another lake house, concealed in its own shade. It's a fair distance away, if one were to walk around the lake's perimeter to reach it, but feels oddly close from where I stand across the water. Chances are, on a Friday afternoon like this, most other houses and cabins up here are vacant. I search the rest of the lake's perimeter, at least what I can see of it, and spot no other properties. None visible, anyway.

When I return my attention to the other lake house, someone is there. My breath catches with surprise. A man paces the lake shore, pausing now and again with his hand over his brow to shield the sunlight as he peers across the lake right toward me. Does he see me, I wonder? I turn rigid. I doubt he can see me. I'm out of the sunlight, standing under the cover of the trees.

It's impossible to tell for sure at such a distance, but I can't help but notice that the man is rather handsome. Or seems to be handsome, anyway. Again, my mind is filling in all the blanks that my long-distance vision leaves.

Without warning, there's a lonesome pang in my heart for Hank. An unexpected feeling. Do I already miss him? Or maybe I'm simply reeling from being alone for the first time in so many years. Truly alone, and not just…

Alone together.

Still shielding his eyes from the sun with one hand, the man across the lake waves to me with his other. My lonely heart skips a beat. He sees me after all, even standing in the gloom like I am. After a prolonged hesitation, I wave back. A fleeting gesture. Another hot flash comes over me. I turn back to the lake house, turn my back on *him*.

Before I even make it back to the porch, I'm dripping with sweat.

TEN

KYLIE

EVEN WITH THE other body gone, Kylie isn't entirely alone. She glimpses a few different critters exploring the basement's shadows while she waits. She spots a mouse tracing the far wall, crawling into view, stopping, twitching its little nose at the air. At one point it seems to spot her and promptly darts out of sight again.

She also sees a spider's web over the stairway, constructed between the boards of the exposed ceiling. It isn't long before she finally sees the spider in question, creeping along the edge of its home, confirming the web is inhabited and not just a dusty cobweb. She also intermittently spots some kind of flying insect buzzing around in the sunlight that comes through the window around the corner—a window she still hasn't seen for herself.

What else is around that corner, anyway, she wonders?

The man—her captor—has been gone for several minutes. She has no idea when he'll be back. She tries to work at her knots again, despite having already tried and gotten nowhere with them. Even with the slender, nimble fingers she has, the knots in the twine are too tight to manipulate. Not to mention she has practically no finger-nails with which to help her. Always a chronic nail biter.

She contemplates exploring the basement anyhow the way she is, with her hands behind her back, her ankles tied together. It'll be difficult but not impossible. She's confident she can hop around well enough.

Before she can try it, however, the house upstairs rattles with the slam of the front door. He's returned. His footsteps move quickly overhead, arriving at the basement door with haste. He yanks the door open, as if he's expecting to catch her in the middle of something. She's exactly where he left her, of course.

Idiot, she thinks.

Despite racing to the basement and nearly pulling it off its hinges, he proceeds to take the stairs nice and slow, one step at a time. There's a certain swagger to his movements Kylie doesn't care for.

Like he thinks he's hot shit, she thinks. *He thinks he's intim-idating.*

And he is. Intimidating. Kylie can't deny she's terrified to find herself in this situation, completely at his mercy. She's also *annoyed* that a monster like him might derive enjoyment from her suffering.

He pauses slightly at the bottom of the stairs. He puts his hands casually into his pockets, appears to admire her, propped against the wall like she is. He strolls closer. Leisurely. He stops a little too close, his crotch practically level with her eyes. She turns away from him, stares intently into the dark corner beside her. From the corner of her vision she sees him crouch down—hears both of his knees pop with the effort.

"What a pretty thing you are," he says, in that chillingly ordinary voice of his. She resists looking at him still. "You remind me a bit of my late wife…"

Kylie's stomach turns over. Somehow she can feel his eyes moving over her, taking her in. She can hardly stand it. She takes a deep breath, doing her best to keep her composure. Then his hand is abruptly on her face. He takes her by the chin and forcefully turns her toward himself. Their eyes meet, his warm and brown. She's never seen him this clearly before, in the brighter light of day—what meager light comes through the basement window. His short salt-and-pepper hair, neatly parted on one side, matches the coloring of his stubble. Kylie hates that it even occurs to her, that her mind is so *of its own* that she can't help thinking how handsome her abuser is. She wants to turn away again, to hide from his ordinary voice and his conventionally attractive face, but he holds her there by the chin, staring deeply into the wells of her eyes, drawing up fear from them by the bucketful and relishing every drop. He turns her face a bit more, studying her every angle. That pit of annoyance in her belly swells. Becomes hatred.

Again, in this moment her mind is entirely of its own.

With a quick twitch of her jaw, Kylie secures the man's thumb in her mouth and bites. Bites *hard.* Her teeth break skin, drawing blood. The man recoils in shock. He jerks his hand away instinctively, reactively, and she peels him against her teeth, drawing more blood still. He pulls free of her, cursing, then strikes her hard with a flat palm, turning her face sharply back where she started, staring into the basement's corner.

"You little bitch."

Kylie watches him from the corner of her eye as he studies his bleeding hand, her face stinging where he slapped her. He leans close to her, close enough she feels his warm breath against her hot cheek.

"You don't seem to appreciate how *awful* I can make this for you."

"No," Kylie says, her voice quavering uncontrollably. "I saw the other girl. I think I got the gist."

"Oh no," the man goes on. "That's only the *half* of it. Just you wait…"

The man stands up again, and a great wave of relief rolls over Kylie, thinking he's about to leave her. Then he places the toe of his boot against her shoulder and shoves her sideways, toppling her onto the cement once more.

"Just you wait," he repeats.

He climbs the stairs and shuts the basement door behind him. Kylie straightens herself out again, wiggling upright with her back against the wall. She watches the basement door with a silent fury in her eyes, chest rising and falling rapidly with her shallow breaths. She's glad he's finally gone… but dreads what will happen when he comes back.

ELEVEN

BARBARA

I'M READING one of my books in the upstairs loft with a bag of Sunchips open in my lap, blindly shoveling them into my mouth as I turn the pages, when suddenly I hear noise above me—a knock, a thump, a scurrying of feet. I look up from my book to the ceiling. I hold my breath to listen. Silence. Then there comes another thump, followed by another. Together, they almost sound like footsteps. Then they stop, and as everything goes quiet again I can't be sure.

My heart is beating fast in my chest.

"What could that be?" I ask aloud, hoping the sound of my own voice will remind me that I'm fine, that *everything* is fine.

There's just someone walking around on the roof, is all.

I set down my book and stand up from the futon, letting all the crumbs I accumulated on my chest rain down to the floor. *Whoops.* I'll clean that up later. I pace the loft with my eyes on the ceiling, until I notice a hatch not much farther from the head of the stairs. The sounds aren't coming from the roof, but the attic over my head. I look around a bit, and it doesn't take much searching to locate the pull-down hook leaned in the corner. I grab it, slender as a golf club in my hand. Whatever's in the attic—*whoever* is in the attic—continues making a bunch of noise as I delicately reach for the curved loop on the underside of the hatch. I successfully hook them both together. I pull, pulling harder as I get a feel for the weight of it. At first it opens slowly, with a lot of resistance, until it abruptly falls freely and the ladder comes sliding down, rattling and hissing. I jump back with a shout as the ladder's rubber feet hit the floor.

"Jesus," I mutter.

I stand and listen for a moment. The sounds in the attic have ceased. Peering up the ladder's steps, I can already tell it's dark up there. I'll need a flashlight. I don't know whether or not I'll find one in Cassidy's lake house, but I *do* know I've got one of my own in the trunk of my car. I fetch my keys from the kitchen counter, hurry out to my car, grab the flashlight from inside my *'Emergency Bag'* and return upstairs to the open attic hatch. In my absence, whatever's up there has begun to shift around again. I hear it bumping and scraping. With the flashlight in one hand, I climb the ladder carefully. It wobbles a little, but it's securely fastened within the hatch's frame. I climb until my head and shoulders rise into the attic's darkness. There I stop. I twist around, juggling the flashlight. I flick its switch and a bright, warm beam shines from its face. I aim it across the attic floor. My heart gives a jolt.

A glossy pair of green eyes sparkle in the flashlight

beam. The raccoon looks at me like a deer in headlights, momentarily paralyzed, before finally it scrambles across the attic floor and escapes through the open gable vent on the other side, where it obviously found its way in. The gable vent appears to open on two hinges, I notice. Like a door. Somehow it got unlocked. Or perhaps a strong wind pulled it open? I have no idea. I shine my light across the wood floor between the vent and the hatch where I'm propped up, trying to decide whether or not I want to crawl through the attic on all fours to close it. I'm leaning towards *no*.

I shine my light elsewhere, a curious sweep, and happen upon some random boxes and what appears to be a *pile of clothes* in the attic's far corner. I squint a little, leaning forward. I see crumpled up jeans, the buttons of several blouses gleaming in the light, and what appear to be some women's trousers. It looks as though Cassidy keeps her excess clothes stored here. Not enough room in her town-house, maybe? As someone whose weight has fluctuated time and time again over the course of my life, I understand what it's like having an entire extra wardrobe I hold onto in hopes of one day fitting into those clothes again.

I decide I'm not going to crawl through the attic. I'll let Cassidy know about the open vent when I return her key on Monday. I'm sure she'll want to know about raccoons rifling through her clothes, possibly nesting in them...

I climb carefully back down the ladder, then take my flashlight downstairs and leave it on the kitchen counter, in case I need it for anything else. As I stand there for a moment, I discover another door in the kitchen I didn't really notice before. A door to the pantry, possibly. I try it, but the knob won't even turn. Locked. Without hesitation, I take the keys out of my pocket and shuffle through them until I'm holding Cassidy's. It's only as I'm about to stick the key into the door that I stop myself.

You shouldn't snoop, I remind myself.

First I'm poking around in the attic, now I'm trying to let myself into the only locked door in Cassidy's lake house. It's only innocent curiosity, I know, but I catch myself feeling guilty all the same.

Either way, it doesn't really matter because when I try to turn the key in the lock, it doesn't budge. Wrong key.

I'd be lying, though, if I said I wasn't even more curious now than before.

TWELVE

KYLIE

She still tastes his coppery blood in her mouth. The saltiness of his skin. The sting of his slap has already faded —the slap itself was nothing to write home about. Kylie's been slapped before. She's been slapped plenty, in fact. Looking past her bindings, and being locked in a strange basement, the slap almost reminds her of home.

Unlike her stinging cheek, however, she's certain the man upstairs still feels her bite. There's something to relish about that, even if it means she'll be punished for it later. Judging by the woman's corpse that preceded her, there's no avoiding such punishment. She's in for some pain, one way or another.

She listens as he stomps about overhead. She hears running water. She imagines him rinsing her saliva from the gouges her teeth made along the base of his thumb, scrubbing his wound frantically as though her bite carries rabies. She hopes she infects him, even if it's just bacterial.

The water shuts off. He stomps around a bit more. He

returns to the basement door and pauses on the other side. If Kylie didn't know better, she'd say he was hesitant to face her again. She tries not to flatter herself.

The basement door opens once more. The man starts down again, his steps more deliberate than last time. He hasn't come empty handed, either. The thing he holds at his side winks and flashes with every other step. Metallic and *pointed.*

He scuffs across the cement and comes to stand before her, holding the knife in plain sight. Try as she might to appear nonplussed, Kylie's heart hammers. She wants to take a deep breath but can't, not without shuddering, without giving away her utter terror. He simply stands there watching her, saying nothing. He tightens and relaxes his grip on the knife's handle. Does he wish to kill her now? Is he that upset about the bite, she wonders?

Before she even considers the repercussions, Kylie asks, "Have you come back to kill me, then?"

He says nothing. He simply considers her that much longer, staring quietly.

"You gonna carve me up like that other girl?" she asks next.

She's not entirely sure why she keeps talking. She regrets every word that tumbles out of her mouth the moment it does, but she can't stop herself. Filling the silence is somehow better than wondering what's about to happen. She also hopes that the boldness of her words will rob him of whatever satisfaction he gains from seeing her frightened.

"Or are you gonna mess around with me a bit first? Hmm? Is that it? Is that what you meant before, about how *awful* you can make this for me? Is that what you do?" She eyes the knife in his hand. She peers into the obscured shadows of his face, sees the deep hollows of his eyes, the vague outline of his nose and mouth. "You some kind of pervert?"

The man shakes his head. "Are you really so foolish? Trying to provoke me like that? In your current predicament? You should be begging for your life."

Despite her inability to take a full breath, Kylie shrugs as nonchalantly as she can muster. "My life sucks. You'll be doing me a favor."

The man makes an amused sort of sound, a puff of air through his nostrils. His handsome mouth grins in the muted dark. He crouches down again, where Kylie can see him better. She glances at the knife in his hand, so dangerously close. Then she studies the hand itself, eyeing the place where she bit him. He's got a large skin-colored bandage over it.

He points the knife her way and she flinches. An involuntary reaction. She hates that she does it all the same, watching as his smile broadens at the sight of her fear. He brings the knife closer to her. She resists pulling away, resists giving him any further satisfaction. Then the knife is in front of her face, its glittering tip quivering delicately. He touches her with it. Its sharp point grazes the shelf of her jaw. She fights the urge to turn her head as he draws the knife up along her cheek, until its cold tip reaches the corner of her mouth. She trembles. A full-bodied reaction.

He lets out another sound of amusement, another puff of breath.

"What an adorably brave face you put on." He tilts his head in observation. "But I can see you're afraid. Your eyes are big. Your breath is shallow. You're practically shivering, and it isn't the least bit cold down here. Yeah, you'll be begging for your life soon enough. They all do."

Kylie finally turns away from the knife against her mouth. She closes her eyes. If she can't fool him, the least she can do is tune him out. One way or another, she'll resist giving him the pleasure he seeks.

Without warning, a sharp pain flares in the bony flesh of her shoulder. Kylie lets out a scream. She jerks in place, slides down the wall in retreat from the man, who holds up the knife between them to admire the prick of blood on its tip. *Her* blood. He's smiling fully now, revealing his handsome, square teeth, his wet tongue glistening between them.

"That's more like it," he says. He laughs softly under his breath as he stands up from his crouched position. "I'll be back to check on you periodically. Be good while I'm gone. Or else."

His smile melts in an instant, his angular face turning to stone as he finally pivots toward the stairs and leaves her. He shuts the basement door behind him. She faintly hears the click of its lock. She listens as his footsteps move around the house upstairs, as the door—what she can only assume is the front door—opens and closes and everything becomes silent again.

THIRTEEN

BARBARA

I'M reluctant to resume my reading in the upstairs loft after the incident with the raccoon. Something about listening to tiny clawed feet crawling around over my head is too distracting, I guess. So instead I gather up a pillow from the bed downstairs, along with a spare blanket from the closet, and I take my book outside to the lake dock. The sun has steadily moved across the sky, pushing the shade of the trees even farther down the dock. The earlier breeze still lives, off and on, off and on, but I don't think it's enough to disturb the pages of my book, or dissuade me from reading outside.

I lay out my blanket near the end of the dock, at the edge of what sunlight is left there. Then I plop down on my belly, using the pillow for cushion under my arms as I prop my book before myself. Not the most comfortable, I'll admit, lying on the rough wood beneath my blanket, but it's comfortable enough. And my book is absorbing enough that I forget any discomfort in just a couple pages.

For a while, at least, with the breeze whispering through the trees around me, cooling the sweat on my brow, I read rather blissfully.

Then I hear the snap of a twig, followed by the crunch of loose soil under someone's boot. I raise my head, roll onto my side, peering down the dock behind me toward the house and my car. That's where I spot him.

The man from across the lake. He's standing by my car, studying my license plate by the look of him.

I set down my book, climb to my feet. I walk softly, planning to surprise him with my presence. Except, as I reach the head of the dock he looks toward me casually as though he already knew I was there. He waves at me in a friendly manner. I was right, before, watching him from across the water. He *is* incredibly handsome.

"Can I help you?" I ask.

I stop once my feet leave the dock, leaving a considerable distance between us.

"Hiya!" he says. He notices I've stopped, notices my crossed arms, as well as the wary look on my face. "Sorry, I don't mean to intrude. I was just taking a lap around the lake, which I like to do a couple times a day, and noticed your car here. Is this your place?"

It feels like a rhetorical question. I shake my head. "No, a friend of mine loaned me her key for the weekend."

The man nods in agreement. I flare with annoyance, privy to the fact that he meant to test me with his question.

"I know the family who owns this place," he says, admitting as much. "I didn't recognize your car, and…" He pauses, laughs. "I guess I just wanted to make sure nobody was here who shouldn't be."

"What a thoughtful neighbor you are," I say. My voice is thick with sarcasm, but gentle enough to be taken as a friendly joke. Or so I hope.

The man shrugs, grimacing with what I interpret to be self-awareness. "I try."

"Is that your place over there, then?" I say, and thumb in the direction of the house across the lake, where I'd first spotted him.

"Yep, that's me!" He sticks his hands in his pockets, rolling from heel to toe in an idle manner. "I've owned property on this lake for... going on *three decades,* now."

He straightens suddenly, as if remembering himself, and starts toward me with an outstretched hand. I can't help but tense a little as he comes. He's still a stranger to me, and I'm alone. But as he gets closer, and I see the warmth of his expression, and the apologetic furrow of his brow, I feel myself soften some.

"I'm Sterling, by the way."

He reaches me, his hand still outstretched, and I notice a thick, skin-colored bandage around the base of his thumb. I'm tempted to ask what happened, or comment, but I don't. I take his hand and shake. His grip is strong. Warm. I feel the tiniest inkling of another hot flash coming on, and try willing it away, wishing for it to die half-born, but it comes full strength like always. By the time I release Sterling's hand I'm sweating again, red in the face.

"Barbara," I reply.

"Well, it's nice to meet you, Barbara." He doesn't let on

that he notices I've broken into a sudden, drenching sweat. I swear, my hot flashes come on at the worst of times so that even I'm confused by them. "Sorry, I didn't mean to interrupt your reading."

"You're fine," I say. An obligatory statement. My eyes are repeatedly drawn all over his face—along his strong, scruffy jawline and his freshly cut salt-and-pepper hair. I fear he catches me taking him in. I take a step back, signaling my return to said reading. "Hopefully I passed the intruder check."

Sterling laughs, a guilty self-deprecating look in his eyes.

"That you did," he says. "I'll let you get back to it, then. Enjoy the rest of your weekend!"

"Thanks."

I give him a polite wave as he turns and continues on his way. By the direction he's going, he truly means to walk an entire lap around the lake, it seems. Kudos to him. I feel a slight pang of shame as I realize that I have no intention of utilizing these beautiful outdoors in such a way—that I fully planned to vegetate all weekend with my books and snacks. I didn't *need* to come to a place like this in order to do the things I'm doing. But now I'm being too hard on myself. And besides, I've still got two days ahead of me. Maybe I'll take a walk around the lake tomorrow and see what all the fuss is about.

For now, I return to my blanket on the dock. I lay down once more, take up my book with my elbows pressed into my pillow. I read two sentences before I gaze distractedly across the lake at the other lake house. I glance the other way, in the direction Sterling must now be tracing the lake's perimeter.

I didn't much care for his visit. I came here to be alone, to be *left* alone. Is that so much to ask? Is it really so difficult to just leave people alone? I'm not entirely sure I buy his excuse that he came to check on his neighbor's things because he didn't recognize me. I think he's nosy. He's also incredibly handsome, even if he must be ten years my senior.

I'm hit with that same longing as before. I miss Hank. I almost wish he was here with me, to enjoy this place. Of course, that would defeat the purpose of this little excursion.

In an attempt to put all these things out of my head, I bury my attention into the pages of my book once again.

FOURTEEN

KYLIE

For a long while, Kylie sits in a stunned stupor.

Her shoulder aches where he stuck her. Her shirt is damp with blood, impossible to see the wound itself through the fabric, as well as with her hands tied behind her back. She wonders how bad it is. How deep. It hurts, but it's nothing compared to what she knows is coming. She repeats his final words in her mind.

Be good while I'm gone. Or else.

When she knows the result will always be the same—that what he ultimately has in store for her will never change—she can't help thinking there's no point in compliance.

"Fat chance," she says at last, and begins struggling to stand.

She pushes herself against the wall to keep her balance as she wobbles onto her feet. She eyes the door at the top of the stairs, which she knows to be locked. Then she eyes the corner ahead. There is still daylight coming through the window around the corner, but not as bright as before.

Keeping to the wall, she begins to hop. Her feet scuff and thump the cold cement. The immediate basement around her is entirely empty. Bare walls, nothing. She expects to find more of the same around the corner. More nothing. After all, she's not the first victim to find herself down here. Probably countless others. She's not the first victim to hop around like this, either. She's not the first to explore these confines in search of something with which to save herself. The man knows what he's doing because he's done it so many times before. He knows he's safe to leave her alone here like this.

But there's nothing else to be done, so why not try, at least?

She nears the corner. She leans her shoulder against it, taking little hops, until finally she's leaned against the sharp angle of the corner itself and the basement beyond is revealed to her. It's *almost* more of the same. Mostly nothing. But there is a single metal shelf standing in the opposite corner of the far wall. The shelf holds what appears to be some rope, some duct tape, and a plethora of dirty pink towels and washrags. It takes a moment for it to sink in.

They're not really pink washrags.

They're stained. Once upon a time those washrags were red. Rinsing them, however, has left them a lovely pale shade of rose.

What Kylie's gaze fastens to next is even worse. In the middle of the floor here, the cement is also stained. Stippled. Splashed. Smeared. The dried blood has turned to a dark, rusty color. She looks up from the stained floor to the ceiling overhead, where she finds a curious addition mounted to the boards there. A metal hook, perfect for stringing someone up off the ground in order to be bled. Even leaning against the cool wall, she feels the strength in her legs give out, as she becomes trembly, her heartbeat becoming tremendously fast.

She can't stay here, she thinks.

It's the most obvious thought a person could have in this situation. And a *worthless* thought, at that. If the women before her couldn't find a way to escape, how does she stand a chance? How is she any different?

The window letting in all the light is too small and too high on the wall to be of any use to her. Its glass is dusty and obviously hasn't been touched in years.

She focuses on the shelf again. On the pink rags, the duct tape, the rope. There's something else on the very top. Something she overlooked before. She spies what appears to be a shiny red toolbox. Classic. Her desperation pushes aside all thoughts of hopelessness, all logic. Her mind instantly fills with *what ifs* and *maybes*. Maybe there's something in that toolbox that could help. Maybe something to cut her binds, to free herself. Maybe a small hammer she could use to break the lock or the knob on the basement door. In an instant she forgets all the victims who came before. She forgets the man's confidence in leaving her alone like this.

Gritting her teeth, Kylie hops across the empty space, across the dried blood beneath the hook that protrudes from the ceiling. She arrives at the shelf, collides against it with all her weight as she uses it to keep from toppling over. She turns her back to it, grabs its frame with her hands behind her back to steady herself. The shelf rattles and wobbles. It's not very sturdy. Without any means of reaching for the toolbox, she shakes the shelf's frame, simultaneously using it to hold herself upright as she throws her weight back and forth. It rocks gently. Surprisingly, the toolbox doesn't move. She grabs hold of the shelf a bit more firmly. Leaning forward, she jerks it toward herself, hoping to rock it a bit more. Instead she simply manages to drag the entire thing squealing and grating across the concrete. The toolbox remains on its top shelf, undisturbed.

"What the hell..." Kylie mutters under her breath.

The toolbox must be heavy, she thinks. She pulls the shelf again. It slides again, nearly a foot away from the wall now.

Upstairs, the front door opens and slams.

Kylie freezes. She cranes her neck to stare directly at the ceiling, at the footsteps that groan right over her head. Those footsteps travel quickly, beelining for the basement door like they always do. Kylie pushes away from the shelf, hops toward the opposite wall, to the jutting corner once more. Hurrying, trying to glide along the next wall back toward her starting place, she loses her balance and spills onto the floor, lands on her shoulder with a painful *whoomp*. The basement door opens. The man's footsteps pound down the steps. He appears before her, lying in the middle of the floor, obviously not where he left her.

"Exploring, huh?"

He looms over her. His boots scuff the cement before her, close enough she can eye the dirt clinging to the soles. He peers beyond her, toward the window and shelf, where he must notice the shelf has been dragged away from the wall, not to mention a handful of washrags that fell to the floor during her exercise.

"Find anything interesting? Hmm?"

Before Kylie can even think to move or speak, he swings the toe of his dirt-crusted boot into her stomach. What little air was left in her lungs shrieks out of her. She crumbles in on herself. With her hands behind her back, she can't even try to shield herself before the next kick comes. She gasps. Her stomach seems to twist and burn. He shoves her over onto her back, drops to his knees, straddling her. He hunches over her. His scent—the earthy musk of his sweat, along with some spicy fragrance which must belong to his deodorant or cologne—fills her nostrils. He clamps his hands around her throat, nearly crushes her with his grip. Already emptied of her breath, she immediately feels it, the struggle, the terrible sensation of bursting from within. A fire in her chest. Her blood pounds in her skull. Beneath the drumming she hears his laughter in her ears. Surely this isn't it, she thinks. Surely this isn't how he intends to finish her off. Unless…

Unless the woman before her met the same fate? Maybe this is how he does it. The cutting comes after. She'll be spared that torture, at least. She'll be dead before he starts—

Through his laughter, through the throbbing pressure in her chest, in her lungs, behind her eyes, she hears another sound. A high-pitched melody. A jingle. All at once, he releases her. Gagging, she sucks down the most painful breath she's ever breathed. The man pulls something from his pocket and the electronic jingle stops as he puts the phone to his ear. He remains straddling her.

"I'm busy right now," he says. "What do you want?"

Still sucking down air, Kylie attempts to scream but all she can manage is a strained croak. Her mind is still swimming in a near-unconscious soup, dizzy, full of fog.

"Okay, but wait a second, I thought…"

The man stands up finally, stepping off of Kylie, pacing toward the foot of the basement stairs. Kylie stretches out on her back. She tries for another scream but can't manage it. She watches as he climbs the basement stairs, with nary a glance behind him to see her on his way out. She is nothing. Already forgotten.

"Then what are you asking me, exactly?"

The basement door shuts. The lock turns. Kylie lays in a heap of exhaustion and frazzled terror, her thoughts spiraling between despair and some other hideous sensation, something akin to violation—knowing just how easily he could have killed her just now. Ended everything.

Suddenly her previous bravery registers as a distant, foreign feeling. An alien concept. Rebellion is another word for naivety.

Breath rasping in the back of her throat, Kylie curls in on herself and begins to sob.

FIFTEEN

BARBARA

I DREAM about my daughter often. Most nights, really, I'd say. Or at least the nights that I remember my dreams. And aside from the nightmares I have about her funeral, usually when I dream of her she's just a kid again. It's rare that I dream of her as she really was before she died. A teenager. A young woman. Almost an adult. No, usually she's still a kid in my dreams, only standing as tall as my shoulder or less. I don't know why. Is it because those are my fondest memories of her? I don't think that's the case. I have so many fond memories of her at every age, at every stage. That can't be it.

When she started growing up, and I mean *really* growing up, making new friends, learning to drive, all that good stuff, she never became too cool for her parents. That *phase* never happened. So I have plenty of amazing memories with my daughter grown, all the time we shared together—the late movie nights, the special-occasion pedicures, the frequent trips to our local bookstore, and the hundred other things we so loved doing together.

But still, when it comes to dreams, something in my mind chooses the older memories. The younger memories.

I wonder if it's because, back in those days, I was more in control of my daughter's safety. She wasn't so independent. There is a certain comfort in that, as a parent. Being in control of the one you care about most. Knowing they're safe because you're the one keeping them safe. You have to let go of that comfort eventually. And it's scary. Not many people talk about how scary it is. At least, not in my circles they never did.

When I have dreams of *that night*—the night I had no control over what would ultimately happen—it's almost as good as any nightmare. It's scary. *Terrifying.* Mostly because I already know what's going to happen, even in the dream. I know how everything will play out, and yet I allow it to play out just the same. I let her go. Every time.

She tells me she's going out with friends. There's a car full of them waiting in the driveway. I spend a minute discreetly watching as my daughter climbs into that car, as the car pulls out into the street, the headlights sweeping across me where I stand at the window, and finally pulling away into the distance until the red taillights are gone, until my daughter is gone. Then I stand at that window for a while longer, knowing she's never coming back.

I wake up to a strong breeze and the sound of the tree creaking over the dock. I blink my eyes. I lift my heavy head off the pillow. My book is lying shut with no book-mark in place to mark my spot because I'd simply dropped it while accidentally falling asleep.

"Oh my God," I murmur drearily.

I can't believe I fell asleep. I squint up into the sky and already I can't see the sun, for it's moved beyond the trees over my head. The sky's clouding up a bit too. Across the lake, over the horizon there, a great mass of clouds looks to be coming in, a little grayer than I'd expected on a day like this. Is it going to storm?

I still can't believe I fell asleep.

I sit up, push myself upright with an old woman's groan. I'm not an old woman, I know. Not old enough to be groaning like this, anyway. Though I am aching in a few places from falling asleep on the hard dock. Despite how poorly I sleep at night, I'm also not usually one for naps...

It's time to head in. Actually, I have no idea what time it is, which is all the more reason to collect my things and head back. I stand up, grab the pillow and my book, pull the blanket into my arms, wrapping it up against myself as I cross the dock and start toward the house, nestled and pretty with dapples of sunlight coming through the trees.

The front door is wide open.

I slow, caught by surprise. The door isn't just ajar, but completely open. I didn't leave it open, did I? Certainly not on purpose. I approach with what feels like overblown caution at first, but I remind myself that, while I might be alone at Cassidy's lake house, I'm not necessarily *alone* up here. I look over my shoulder in the direction of Sterling's house across the lake. Not that I suspect him of snooping around inside Cassidy's lake house while I napped… but I also know nothing about the man, so who am I to assume one way or another?

The porch steps creak as I climb them. The porch itself gives a little groan as I approach the front door. I listen in the open doorway. The house is entirely quiet.

"Hello?" I call out. I feel silly for it. But again, just in case.

I proceed to conduct a half-thorough investigation of the house, checking each of the rooms, the loft upstairs, the bathroom downstairs. I check the main bedroom where my bag still sits open on the bed. Nothing appears to be disturbed. Nothing I can see at first glance, anyway. Most likely I failed to close the front door and the breeze pushed it wide open. Perfectly plausible.

As I stand at the foot of the bed, a strange sensation comes over me. A sense of being *watched*. I feel it in my shoulders, the back of my neck. I tense up. I turn slightly, and from the corner of my eye I see the bedroom closet beside me. Someone is there. I don't know where this feeling is coming from. It hits me hard for a moment. A terrible certainty. But as I stand and watch those closet doors, my logical brain catches up with my animal one, and I ask myself: *do I really believe someone could be standing inside that closet, watching me?*

More likely I'm being paranoid. Skittish. I'm not used to being alone like this. Even if I've been *lonely*, Hank has always been with me, in another room of the house at the very least. Perhaps the solitude of this place is getting to me.

I break free of the spell that keeps me rooted in place. I go to the closet, slow on my feet. It's a set of sliding doors. I grab the left side, the door on the outer track, and after a brief pause I pull it rumbling open, my breath held tight.

It's only when it's open and I'm faced with its dark *emptiness* that I realize I had no real plan, nothing in hand to defend myself with if there *had* been someone waiting inside. Oh well. I'm lucky, I guess. I sigh a breath of relief.

This is my first time looking inside this particular closet. There are clothes on hangers inside. I shuffle through them, mostly long sleeves, sweaters, a couple jackets. Winter attire. These are definitely things Cassidy would wear. She must not have enough space at her place for all her clothes and swaps them out here during the change of seasons, I assume. I'm reminded again of the clothes I found in the attic, a whole pile of women's attire. Cassidy must have a clothes shopping addiction. Not unheard of.

I notice something else, on the shelf over the hanging rack. A small box. At first glance I think it's a shoebox. It's the right size. Upon closer examination, however, I can see that it's a wooden box, painted a lovely lilac purple.

Am I snooping again? Am I *a snoop?* I've never considered myself one, but then again I'm already on my tiptoes and the wooden box is already in my hands. I pull it down. It's a rectangular wooden box, blank, no engraving or anything etched on its lid. I set it down on the bed. I don't open it right away. Instead I rest my hands on either side of its lid and ask myself again: *Am I really going to snoop through Cassidy's things?*

A sticky wave of guilt creeps over me. Or maybe it's just another hot flash.

I lift the lid off the wooden box and set it aside. Inside is a collection of folded up notes. A few dozen, at least. I absolutely should *not* be looking at this, or invading Cassidy's privacy in this manner, especially not after she was kind enough to let me stay here, free of charge. And yet I still can't get a hold on my curiosity. It's compulsory. I take out a note. I unfold it gently, revealing the neat handwriting inside. A letter. It begins with *'Dear Cass.'* Before reading anything in the letter's body, I skip to the end to see who it's from. It's signed, *'Love, Mom.'* Out of growing curiosity, I grab another and check its contents. It's the same. I check a third note. The same again. These are all letters to Cassidy from her mother. I decide to read a little from the one currently in my hands.

It reads:

Dear Cass,

I miss you so much, it's impossible to put into words. I wish things were different. I wish I could see you. I hope you're getting my letters. I can't say too much here, but I hope you know just how much I love you. I hope you know you'll always be my darling little...

. . .

I lower the letter in my hands as I hear what sounds like a car door slamming shut outside. I hurry to the bedroom window, discreetly pull the blinds apart, and flinch as my heart jumps into my throat.

Cassidy?

She's outside, her car parked next to mine, making her way toward the front porch.

I race back to the wooden box. I fold the letter up as quickly as I can, stuff it back inside with the rest, replace the lid, and return the box to the shelf in the closet. I slide the closet door shut just as I hear a loud series of knocks on the front door. I look frantically over the room, make sure nothing else is out of place. Of course nothing is—it was only the box from the closet, which I've put back just as I found it. Yes. That's everything. There's nothing else for me to be concerned about.

And yet, as I make my way out of the bedroom, my heart is still pounding.

I take a deep breath before I answer the door.

"Hello!" Cassidy says, smiling big and wide-eyed. She's standing on the doormat with something in either of her hands—a plastic-wrapped plate in one, and what looks like a bottle of wine in the other.

"Cassidy!" I try to match her enthusiasm. "Hello! I... I wasn't expecting you..."

"I know, I'm sorry," she says. "I tried texting you first, but I never got a reply..."

This makes sense, considering I've made a concerted effort not to look at my phone too much since my arrival.

"I'm not going to stay, don't worry. I just wanted to

make sure everything here was good and you were settling in all right. *And...*" She holds out the gifts in her hands. "... I thought I'd swing by after work to bring you a little *somethin' somethin'*."

"Oh my goodness," I say, wearing my biggest, most gracious smile. "You really shouldn't have."

Cassidy looks at me strangely, her head tilted to one side. "Is everything okay? You look like you've been working up a sweat or something."

I open my mouth to answer, but I'm not sure what to say. Finally I force a laugh.

"Oh, it's nothing, really. I get these annoying *hot flashes,* you know. Just part of getting older. They come at the most random of times, I swear."

I honestly can't tell if this is a hot flash, or burning shame for having nearly been caught snooping through Cassidy's things. But for the sake of quelling Cassidy's concern, I use the easy excuse. She seems to accept it. She pouts her lips sympathetically.

"It must be miserable this time of year, when it's already so hot," she says.

"Oh, you have no idea." I offer an appreciate laugh.

Cassidy extends her gifts again. "I brought you some wine and a plate of goodies to help make your first night a little more special—some chocolate chip cookies and some chocolate chunk brownies. This is the *good* stuff. Nothing from a box."

Naturally. I can't deny Cassidy's baking has always been on point. Irresistible. I take both the wine and the plate, then stand aside to welcome her into the lake house.

Her lake house. She bows her head meekly as she steps inside, as if flattered that I've accepted her company. I don't really have a choice. Not that I'm *unhappy* with her visit or anything…

"So, what do you think of the place?" she says. She looks around, likely noticing that everything is exactly where she last left it. I haven't done a whole lot to make myself at home, besides putting my groceries in the fridge and dumping my bag in the bedroom. "It's cute, right?"

I make my way to the kitchen counter, where I set the wine and baked goods.

"It's more than cute," I answer. "You were right. This whole area is gorgeous. It really is."

"Right? I've been coming here for years, so it's easy to take it for granted sometimes. But even still, every time I drive around that last bend and this place comes into view, I just *melt*. Like, instant relaxation."

"I took a book out on the dock earlier—I thought it'd be nice to read a little, with the sun and the trees and everything—and it *was* nice. A little too nice, actually." I laugh. "I had myself a little nap…"

Cassidy bursts out laughing, genuinely pleased to hear I'm enjoying myself. I burn a little more inside, prickling with shame for going through her things.

"I bet that was satisfying," she says. "Though, unless you brought some bug spray, I don't recommend it after sundown. I'm afraid there's a bit of a mosquito problem."

I haven't been bothered by many insects, but her mentioning of mosquitos does remind me of one pest— although maybe it's entirely unkind to refer to him as such.

"I did get to meet your neighbor," I say, broaching the subject with possibly the worst segue I can imagine. "Sterling?"

Cassidy rears her head back in surprise. She furrows her brow. "Oh. Really? That's... kind of strange."

"He stopped by unexpectedly. He seemed to know you. Or your family, anyway."

Cassidy turns her head, gazing pensively toward the front door—or more generally, the direction of Sterling's house across the lake.

"I mean, yeah. I've met him before. But it's a little weird he came by like that. Did he happen to say why?"

"It was while I was reading on the dock. I don't think he meant anything by it. He said he was out walking a lap around the lake and... well, I think he just wanted to make sure I wasn't someone who didn't belong."

I laugh a little, trying to come across as less concerned than I am, but Cassidy still frowns in a funny way.

"Huh," she says. "Interesting."

"So it's true? He knows your family?"

After a moment of distracted contemplation, Cassidy nods. "Yeah. I think he's owned that place as long as we've owned this one. He's an okay guy. I don't think you need to be worried or anything. I'm just a little surprised he stopped by like that, is all."

At the very least, I'm relieved that Cassidy agrees it's strange—that my recent anxieties weren't wholly unfounded. I'm also relieved to hear that it sounds like he's mostly harmless, even if there's always still that chance with strangers.

"Yeah, I'm not really worried," I lie. "I just thought I'd better mention it. Just in case."

"No, for sure. I'm glad you did. And you're welcome to call me, too, if you're ever concerned about anything. Like, *anything.* I'm not that far." She gives me a comforting look. "Anyway, I don't want to keep you! I'm glad you like the place. I just wanted to stop by to see if you needed anything, and to bring you something to make your first night a little more *decadent.*"

She gives me a devious, knowing little smirk as she turns for the door. After all these weeks and months bringing goodies into the office, and my complete inability to resist them, she knows better than anyone we share that same weakness. That same *vice.*

"Thank you," I say. "Again. Really. Not just for the wine and cookies, but for everything. This has already been great. I'm looking forward to another two days here."

The mere thought actually sparks a pang of dread in me. Can I handle another two days? Alone? With nothing to keep me company but my books? It sounds silly, but I'm not accustomed to so much free time.

"You deserve it," Cassidy says. She lingers in the doorway, clasping and unclasping her hands, and I can tell she's aching to give me a hug before she leaves. At last, in a desperate bid she throws open her arms and comes at me, and after everything I've just said, I'm rather helpless to refuse it. I hug her in kind. Short but sweet. As soon as we separate, Cassidy moves through the doorway and onto the front porch. She looks back as she walks, points a stern finger at me, and says, "You've got my number! Don't hesitate to call me if you need something. Anything at all."

"Of course," I say. "Thanks again, Cassidy."

She offers me one last over-the-shoulder smile before she takes her keys out from her pocket on her way down the porch steps toward her car. I watch as she climbs behind the wheel and the engine starts, and she waves through the windshield at me. Or I think she does, it's hard to tell with the sun-soaked reflection of the leaves in the trees across the glass. I wave from the doorway, just in case.

Then she pulls out and drives off. I'm alone again.

I shut the door and stop there a spell, just standing and staring into nothing as I replay the whole interaction in my head—her kindness, my paranoia, her complete obliviousness to my snooping through her things mere seconds before her arrival.

I remember myself. I turn to face the house, the kitchen, the countertop where Cassidy's treats await me. I'm tempted to unwrap them now and help myself, to give me that chocolatey dopamine hit and ward off all these guilty feelings in me. But I resist for now.

I think I'll make a whole evening of it instead.

SIXTEEN

KYLIE

KYLIE LAYS EXACTLY where the man left her for a long while. Her tears have since dried on her cheeks, and the bruises on her throat have already darkened to a deep purple. She feels the sharp ache in her ribs where she was kicked and absentmindedly wonders if his kicks broke anything. She doesn't dare move again. Not now. Not yet. Not just because it'll probably hurt when she does, but because she doesn't wish to be found out of place again.

The fight has gone out of her.

Was it worth it, she wonders? Running away? Obviously not. She'd give anything to go back, to endure her lame drunk of a father and all his grotesque, leering friends. Anything would be better than this. Her father has no idea she's even here. No one does. No one knows she's even missing, she thinks. Her father has probably already washed his hands of her. Her sister never even knew to expect her. Kylie is just *gone*, and the world has no idea.

The world could not care less.

Her eyes burn with emotions. Emotions she doesn't wish to explore right now. Not ever. What's the use, anyway? What's the use in feeling sorry for herself at a moment like this? When it's hopeless?

Let me wake up. Let this all be a stupid nightmare.

Stupid is right. She was stupid to quit her shitty little job. She was stupid to run away. She was stupid to climb inside that car. If anything, she *deserves* all of this just for being so damned *stupid*. She regrets everything. She wants nothing more than to wake up, for none of this to have happened, to go back to her shitty little job, her shitty father, all of it. She'd take that shitty life back in a heartbeat just to be alive in it.

The basement transforms as she lays on the hard concrete. The meager light from the window dims, burns warm and red, then dims further, turning dark with night-fall. Deep shadows pool into the corners of the room, flood across the cement, drowning Kylie as they come.

Still she lies just as he left her.

The door above slams shut. Her tormentor's footsteps clomp and scuff about aimlessly. Soon his movements bring him to the door atop the stairway. It unlocks. Pulls open. Kylie rolls her weary eyes toward the doorway and watches his descent. He arrives at the foot of the stairs with something in his grasp. Sharp and slender, it catches the scarce moonlight along its sleek surface. She turns rigid at the sight of it.

Not again.

The man moves toward her silently. That obnoxious swagger has found its way back into his gait. False confidence. Performative. He stops beside her, so that all she can see of him are his legs. He lowers the knife at his side, so she sees that, too, vibrating beside his leg because he grips it so tight.

Because he's full of rage.

He stands there for quite some time, saying nothing. She says nothing right back. She doesn't dare. She trusts him now, what he said before:

You don't seem to appreciate how awful I can make this for you.

She appreciates his words. Fully.

"Not yet," he mutters under his breath. She barely hears it. He's whispering to himself. "Not yet. Too soon…"

He turns on his heel and returns to the stairs. He stomps his way back up. The basement door shuts. The lock clicks.

She's alone again.

She lets out a breath of relief.

SEVENTEEN

BARBARA

THE SUN'S GOING DOWN. The storm over the lake is now over *me*, over Cassidy's lake house, darker than it was before, threatening rain but delivering nothing so far.

I'm trying to read my book in the loft again—no more noises in the attic, thankfully—but my mind is repeatedly distracted by its own thoughts.

I keep thinking about my phone downstairs on the nightstand. I keep wondering if Hank has perhaps texted me anything all day. I've deliberately stayed *off* my phone, knowing how easy it is to find myself scrolling, thinking about all the same things I think about most days, the things I came here to avoid for a time. But the longer I go without it, the stronger the urge becomes, until I can hardly concentrate on anything else. I've read the same page three times over now.

I finally set my book down. I sigh with defeat.

My phone is waiting for me facedown on the night-stand. For a moment before I pick it up, I'm tempted to leave it there, to truly test my willpower. But who am I kidding? I snatch it off the nightstand and check the lock screen. As it turns out, I have received messages from Hank. All at once my little heart sings. My stomach swells with butterflies.

His text, sent two hours ago, reads: *Hope you're enjoying the first day of your relaxing getaway! I've already got my extra large pizza order submitted for my solo pig-out. Love you.*

I'm grinning from ear to ear. I catch myself doing it, aware of myself entirely, and I can't help thinking how dumb this entire thing is—all my anxiety regarding my *'failing marriage.'* It's not failing at all. Maybe *I've* been failing. Maybe *we've* been failing. But not our marriage. Our marriage is fine. Our marriage *will be* fine. Hank's message fills me with an odd relief, to know that I'm not the only one potentially enjoying our time apart.

I type out my reply: *I already miss you.*

I stop myself from sending it. I read it a few times over, unsure. Then I delete it. That's not what I want to send him. I think of something else.

We should do something like this together sometime.

That's better. It *feels* better. Even if my initial words were true, I'm not sure now is the best time for them.

I hit SEND.

I stand for a bit just staring at my phone, anticipating his reply any second, as if he's just standing at the ready, waiting all day for me to get back to him. I'm being foolish. I place my phone on the nightstand again, screen down. It's time to ignore it some more. Allow myself to be disconnected.

Curious about the developing storm, I step out onto the front porch. The sun is completely below the horizon now, dropping the lake into a fuzzy, gray-blue shadow. The clouds I can see across the water are darker than ever. The breeze has blown in some cool air, sweet with the smell of a storm fit to burst any second. It probably wouldn't be a good idea to read on the dock again, but here, on the porch, it feels lovely. If it does begin to sprinkle, I'll be safe on the steps. The thought of sitting here with my book and a glass of wine and Cassidy's cookies beside me sounds too divine to pass up. In fact, I'm practically giddy as I return inside to fetch my things. I grab the same blanket and pillow as before, then the wine and cookies from the kitchen counter. I have no idea if Cassidy's got any wine glasses in her kitchen cupboards, but I don't even bother checking. Just the bottle will do. I search the drawers in the kitchen until I find a corkscrew.

I take everything onto the dark porch. I set the plate of baked goods and the bottle of wine on the top step, where I sit and drape the blanket across my legs, then unwrap the plate of goodies and take a deep breath of their aroma. God, I love the smell of chocolate chip cookies. I set them aside, then make quick work of the wine cork. I take a whiff of the wine as well, a delicious red, and practically shudder with excitement. I don't even wait. I tip the bottle to my lips. Call me a heathen, I don't care. I couldn't care less about letting it *breathe.* It can breathe in my stomach. After my first guzzle, I cradle the bottle in my lap and peer across the dark clearing toward the lake. The leaves in the trees whisper beautifully around me. That cool-yet-still-humid breeze sweeps across me, swirling about the porch. I put the wine to my lips again and take another swig.

As I lower the bottle a second time, I notice something in the nearby trees. Lights in the dark. Tiny, floating, yellow-green lights. *Fireflies.* They bob languidly through the shadows. The wine in my belly turns warm as I watch them. Then another light appears, this one violently brief in the clouds over the water in the far distance. A few seconds later, the low, rumbling thunder rolls over my head. I focus on the fireflies, take another sip of wine.

God, this is nice...

I remember when my daughter was very young— maybe five or six—and we watched fireflies together for the first time. Hank explained to her that you could pinch off a firefly's backside and smear the luminescence on yourself, but even at such a tender age our daughter was horrified by the thought, understanding that the fireflies were living things, too, and not simply our disposable playthings...

Lost in these memories, I'm suddenly distracted by a *third* source of light. Not fireflies or lightning in the distance, but a bright beam swinging through the dark through the trees on my left. Someone's flashlight. I stiffen, squeeze the neck of the wine bottle tight in my grasp. The flashlight beam hovers around the curve of the lake, into my clearing, until at last its wielder is revealed behind it.

It's Sterling again, I'm quite sure. Another lap around the lake? At this hour? As he crosses the clearing, he doesn't appear concerned with me or Cassidy's place. Sitting in the dark like I am, I'm fairly certain he doesn't even realize I'm out here.

I'm overcome with the urge to startle him if I can.

I set down the wine bottle. I wait until he nears the lake dock, passing in front of it, and cup my hands to my mouth.

"You weren't kidding about those walks, huh?"

He comes to an abrupt halt, straightens from head to heel. I can't stop myself from sniggering at his expense. He aims his light in my direction, bright as a spotlight on Cassidy's porch. I squint, still laughing softly.

"Wow," he says, and laughs as well. "Way to frighten an old man half to death."

"Oh, you're not that old," I say.

God, this wine went to my head fast.

He makes his way toward me, shaking his head with playful disapproval. He points his flashlight down a little, so as not to aim it directly into my face.

As he notices the bottle of wine beside me, he says, "You look like you're having quite the night."

Another bout of thunder rolls overhead. He cranes his neck toward the sky as he continues making his way toward me.

"Might get rained on here pretty soon…"

He stops at the foot of the porch steps, close enough I'm able to once more admire just how well-proportioned he is. He looks at me for a prolonged moment, until I realize I'm staring. Or maybe we're both staring. A swelling, raging hot flash burns me up from the inside out. Why are they always so ill-timed? I avert my eyes. Eager to play it cool, I reach for the plate of cookies beside me and extend them toward Sterling, anything to fill the silence.

"Cookie?" I say.

"Oh," he says, eyeing the plate.

"Surely you've burned enough calories today, with all your walking, to afford a cookie or two."

"Or two?" he says, with a laugh.

"If you don't take a couple, I'm afraid I'll eat them all myself. You'll be doing me a favor."

"Well, then," he says, reaching for the plate. "Don't mind if I do…"

He takes a single cookie. He smells it before taking a bite, then turns to see the lake at his back. Lightning continues to flash in the far distance. Soft thunder burbles across the sky. I watch him discreetly while he's turned away from me, the way the muscles in his jaw bulge with each chew, under his salt-and-pepper scruff.

Admiring him the way I am, I can't help thinking of Hank again, this time with an aching guilt.

"What brings you out here, anyway?" Sterling asks, turning to face me again. He pushes the rest of the cookie into his mouth and proceeds to speak with a mouthful. "Just needed a quiet place to read, or what?"

"I guess you could say that," I answer. "I just wanted some time alone, really."

"Oh!" Sterling dons a look of apology. "Well, in that case, I'd better take my leave! I don't mean to keep bothering you…"

"Well, to be fair, I shouted at *you*." I extend the plate once more to him. "Please, take another."

He considers the plate for a moment as though conflicted. Then he does as I ask and takes a second cookie.

"These are pretty good," he says. "You make them yourself?"

I hesitate. "Yes."

I don't know why I lie. Maybe because I'm not interested in explaining Cassidy or my relationship with her, or anything else about my stay here. Truthfully, as nice as Sterling is to look at, I'm eager for him to be on his way. I *did* come here to be alone, after all. Not to get wrapped up in small talk. God, how I hate small talk. And yet, I still find myself returning his question anyway, prolonging the interaction.

"Are you here on a break, or do you live out here?"

He takes a bite of his second cookie. Then he takes a deep breath as he chews on both the cookie and the question I've asked.

"I just like to come out here once a month or so… for the solitude." He swallows, and his throat makes an audible *gulp.* "You can really be yourself in a place like this, you know?"

I'm not sure I *do* know, but I nod anyway.

"Anywho," he says, taking another bite of his cookie, "thanks for the mid-walk snack. I'll let you get back to your alone time."

"Of course. Enjoy the rest of your walk. Try not to get rained on."

He glances up at the sky again. "Yeah, we'll see. I might make this a short one. Enjoy the rest of your night, Barbara."

He tips the last of his cookie to me in a friendly sort of salute and returns in the direction he came from. A short walk indeed. I set the plate of cookies down, replace it with the bottle of wine in my hands again. I take another swig.

As soon as Sterling vanishes back into the trees, and the light from his flashlight disappears with him, I'm immediately thinking of Hank. Has he responded to my latest text yet, I wonder?

I set down my wine and hurry inside to find out.

EIGHTEEN

KYLIE

THERE MUST BE something wrong with her, Kylie thinks.

There must be some reason these things keep happening. Not being kidnapped specifically, of course. This is the first time *that's* ever happened. But *bad things*, generally speaking. It's like the world just keeps throwing its worst at her, again and again. She knows there's good out there, too, even if she's seen very little of it. She knows it must exist because other people seem to enjoy it, share inspiring stories about it, brag about it. But in Kylie's seventeen years, the *good* in the world has done a commendable job of eluding her.

Because there's something wrong with me.

It's the reason she's never been able to make any friends. It's the reason her father openly roots against her in all things. It's the reason she's never been any good at anything she's tried, whether in academics or sports or hobbies or whatever else. It's the reason her low-life boss assumed he could get away with the inappropriate jokes, the increasingly invasive touching, or the final straw—propositioning her for sex in exchange for not writing her up when her till came up twenty dollars short on her final night at the theater.

It's the reason Kylie's mother left when she was only six years old.

Obviously something is very wrong with her. Something innate she can't see, but somehow everyone else can. Even the man upstairs can see it, whatever it is. It's why he must have picked her. She's expendable. Forgettable. The world and all its good will not miss her. Maybe it'll even be a better place without her.

One thing in particular that she suspects might be wrong with her—a characteristic she's become quite familiar with over the years—is the fact that these ideas, these *insights,* only serve to make her angrier. She feels sorry for herself for a minute, as is tradition, before suddenly she remembers what a *crock of shit* the world really is, along with all those people who never gave her a chance. A *real* chance. Who are *they* to make assumptions? What did she ever do, to make them think so little of her? What makes *him* so sure that she'll just roll over and take it?

In any case, he's wrong. Kylie stubbornly clings to life not because she's desperate to live it, but because…

"Because fuck 'em," she miserably croaks, her throat still aching from the strangling.

She moves. She twists where she lays, peering up the stairs at the dark face of the basement door. She hasn't heard his movements for some time. It's impossible to say how long—time flies when you're having fun, and all that.

Gingerly, with much gasping and wincing, she sits up. Her ribs ache, but she's not entirely sure they're broken. Maybe just bruised. Is it really possible to tell the difference? Sitting up awkwardly, with her legs bent, her hands eternally attached to the small of her back, she looks around the near-pitch-black basement and wonders what her next possible move might be.

She struggles to her feet, teeters like a poorly planted scarecrow. As she loses her balance, she tosses herself toward the nearest wall and catches herself there. She takes a breath or two. She hops ahead, back to the same corner as before, where she peers into the other half of the cramped basement, the tiny window there letting in the scarcest moonlight. The shelf is exactly where she left it, pulled slightly away from the wall. She hops toward it again. She catches herself dramatically against the side of it, huffing and puffing from her efforts.

"Let's try this again…"

With her back to the shelf, she grasps its frame in both hands and begins to jerk it back and forth. She's a bit more desperate this time around. A little more reckless. She puts all of her weight into it, careless of the mess she might make. Better to do it now and make as much noise as she needs when the man upstairs is seemingly absent. The shelf scrapes and scoots across the cement. Not the intended result. She pushes and pulls at it some more, puts her whole body into the motion, until suddenly the shelf starts to tip. She allows herself to tip with it.

Kylie lets out a pained grunt as she hits the floor, as the shelf loudly bangs to the floor behind her. The toolbox rattles noisily across the cement likewise. Wasting no time, she spots it in the dark, a red gleam, and worms her way toward it. She sits up again, her back to the toolbox lying on its side. She grabs it with both hands, turns it upright. She scrabbles her fingers across its face until she finds it clasp. She pulls the clasp open, lifts it, unfolds it, so that the tool-box's lid can be opened freely. She drags the toolbox closer, lifts the lid open. She shifts and squirms as she sticks her bound hands into its contents.

Gimme something. Anything.

Preferably something with a sharp edge, she thinks. Something she might use to cut through her binds. The twine around her wrists and ankles is fine enough that its knots can't be picked by nimble fingers, but it's also fine enough that any sharp instrument could cut through it potentially, if only she had such a tool.

C'mon, gimme something, please…

She tries to peek at what she rifles through, but it's so dark she can hardly make anything out one way or another. She grabs something long and slender, a plastic handle with a smooth, narrow tool piece. A screwdriver. She drops it, continues digging. She also finds a small hammer, a pair of needle-nose pliers, a whole assortment of screws and metal washers, a wrench, a tiny tape measure. She grabs many of these things multiple times over, confusing them for some-thing new. That's it. That's all there is. Nothing much in the way of *cutting* anything. The most useful thing, she thinks, are the needle-nose pliers. Maybe she can get a grip on the twine with them, break it with pure friction alone.

She twists the pliers around in her hand, careful not to

drop them. It's awkward as hell. She opens them, struggles to keep a grip on the handles as she works to ensure the twine is in the pliers' mouth. She squeezes them closed. She maneuvers them left and right, back and forth, all around in an attempt to strain the twine against the pliers' edges. It's not a tool for cutting, by any means, but she's certain if she keeps at it, she can eventually rub and pinch the twine enough to—

The door upstairs slams shut. Kylie's blood runs cold.

He's back.

NINETEEN

BARBARA

I QUICKLY DISCOVER the wine in my belly has already begun taking effect as I climb to my feet and head inside. I forgot what a lightweight I am. I feel like I'm barely touching the floor, or like I need to be a tad more careful about each step, as my right foot carries me farther rightward than normal, my left foot farther leftward. Or maybe it just feels that way, a matter of perception. I've mostly got a handle on myself again as I start for the bedroom. I'm not drunk, by any means. I've just got a strong buzz, that's all.

I go to the nightstand, where my phone lies facedown. I pick it up compulsively, tap the screen to wake it.

One new text message. It's from Hank. My *strongly buzzed* heart swells with deep longing as I open our text conversation to read his reply.

It reads: *I would love that. I'll even start looking at some resorts now.*

Resorts. Does he mean actual vacation resorts? The mere suggestion is so unlike Hank, I'm immediately struck by the gesture, the clear indication that he's *trying*, that he wants to make this work. So do I. Just reading his text sends my mouth involuntarily grinning from ear to ear. I can hardly stop even if I wanted to. The thought of my husband, my Hank, perusing vacation plans, destination getaways, it's almost too much for me to believe. I laugh a little, with my nose practically buried in my phone.

I want to reply to his text, but I'm not sure what to say. Perhaps I should wait a little. I'm not entirely myself. I don't think I drank *that* much wine, but it's hitting me harder than I expected.

I take my phone with me back to the front porch. I step outside just as another lightning strike strobes against the lake's reflection, illuminating everything in cold, blue, flickering light.

The flash gives me a stark view of the fat raccoon dragging my plate of cookies off the porch steps.

"Hey!"

I stumble after it. The raccoon lets out something like a hiss—garbled and growly. I slide to a stop at the head of the steps, grabbing the porch railing as my tipsy feet threaten to spill me. The plate of cookies tips off the final step, overturning into the dirt at the bottom of the stairs. Heedless of my presence, the raccoon grabs as many treats off the dirt as it can and dashes away. It lets out a series of whimpering grunts as it goes, a grunt for each swing of its backside, which almost sounds like snickering to my ears.

I can hardly believe what I just witnessed. Momentarily stunned, all at once I burst out laughing.

I hold onto the railing with both hands as I can hardly

keep standing, I'm laughing so hard. I give up. I sit down on the top step. I regard the turned over plate on the dirt below and it only makes me laugh that much harder.

As I finally settle down, and the shock of the situation wears off, I take up my bottle of wine and have myself yet another sip. I eye a broken cookie in the dirt and giggle a little more.

I take up my phone again. I read over my husband's last text, the one about researching vacation resorts. I decide not to follow up with anything pertaining to that.

Instead I type out: *You won't believe what just happened.*

TWENTY

KYLIE

"Come on," Kylie whispers. "Come on. Come on..."

The pliers aren't doing anything. They do slip out of her hands, however. She has to pat the ground behind her butt to find them. The man upstairs makes his way to the basement door. What's he going to do, she wonders, when he finds her like this? The shelf tipped over? His toolbox open and its contents all over the floor? What will her punishment be this time? Even as she scrapes the pliers off the cement, she knows it's no use. This was yet another stupid, impulsive series of mistakes she's made. But what was her alternative, exactly? Was she just supposed to sit quietly and wait to die?

The basement door opens. Kylie freezes. She listens as a heavy silence settles over the place. The man seems to stop in the doorway. She can't see him, but knows he must be standing there. His footsteps have yet to creak down the basement stairs. What's he waiting for, she wonders? What is *she* waiting for?

She continues with the pliers. She gets them open again, gets them placed over the twine against her wrists.

The man stomps down the stairs at last. In the flat dark, his shape appears from around the corner, where he finds her sitting in the mess she's made. Kylie peers up into the black hole of his face. Only one part of him catches any light through the window, and it's the knife in his fist.

"What have you been up to?" he says. "Making messes?"

He takes one step and then stops. He reaches outward, puts his hand against the wall to steady himself. Kylie's heart is in her mouth. It's beating so quickly, its thrum causes her sore ribs to ache.

"Oh, God, what's this, then..." the man murmurs beneath his breath.

He hunches for a moment, still bracing himself with one hand, before finally correcting his posture, pushing away from the wall. He approaches her once more. Kylie leans away as he stands right against her, the knife turning dangerously in his grasp. His breathing is heavy. Labored. She's reminded of her father's drunken nights, the way he would lose all control, panting like a bulldog, barely able to stand up straight.

Without a word, the man grabs a handful of Kylie's hair. She screams. He wrenches her, swiveling over the cement, and drags her away from the shelf, away from the toolbox. The pliers fall from her grasp. Her helpless body whispers over the floor, her hair pulled taut by the roots, her scalp screaming for release. He drags her around the corner, back into the darker half of the basement where he releases her in a stiff heap. He towers over her, his shadow barely visible in this deeper dark. He's breathing even harder than before. He starts to crouch beside her but loses his balance. He catches himself, one hand on the ground. He stands up again. Lying on her back, Kylie watches him with terror racing through her veins. Suddenly, however, he hardly seems to notice her at all. Distracted. Unfocused. He touches his head with one hand.

"What is this," he repeats. Then, as something seems to dawn on him, "Oh..."

He staggers to the foot of the stairs, where he catches himself against the wall once again. He doesn't just steady himself with his hand this time, however. He leans his whole shoulder against it and *still* fights to maintain his balance. Even in the dark, Kylie sees the way his legs tremble, threatening to buckle beneath him.

"Shit..."

Without warning, he turns into the corner, jams his hand into the back of his throat, and proceeds to retch. He vomits so badly, he drops his knife, clattering onto the cement beside him. Kylie is still frozen. Bewildered. She peers at the knife. Then she looks to the stairs, to the basement door at the top.

It's wide open.

However slim, now's her chance.

She lunges forward, off her back and onto her knees. She struggles to stand up on her bound feet. She pitches forward, lands hard on her knees again. The man continues to retch in the corner, oblivious to her, oblivious to everything outside himself for the time being. Kylie gets her toes planted on the cold ground, rocks herself backward onto them, rolls onto her feet and stands upright in one fluid, reeling motion. She hops desperately for the stairs. There's no time to try for the knife. Maybe if her hands weren't secured behind her back, she would, but...

The man lets out a terrible, vile cough, wet with sick. Kylie pauses briefly at the foot of the stairs, considers her options. No matter how she does it, it's not going to be easy.

She hops onto the bottom step. She sways there, forward and back, forward and back. She can't keep her balance. She pitches forward onto the rest of the stairs, banging herself up nice and sore in the process. Her aching ribs vibrate. She turns over onto her back, onto her butt, sitting on the third —or fourth?—step. She pushes herself backward with both feet, hopping upward and landing hard on her butt one step at a time.

Down below, her captor arches his back like a cat with a hairball. He retches again. He spits. He looks over his shoulder and scours the dark, finally remembering he's got company. The wooden stairs creak under Kylie's weight. His eyes fasten to her there, nearly to the top. She scoots herself up another step. Then another. She can hardly believe how close she is. The man turns from his sick in the corner, picks up his dropped knife which scrapes shrilly off the cement. He stumbles toward the stairs. He wobbles, using the wall to guide himself.

Kylie's panting so hard now she thinks she might vomit herself.

She reaches the top of the stairs. She pushes herself

across the threshold, through the open door and onto the laminate flooring on the other side. She's in a small, dark hallway. She presses herself against the opposite wall there, uses it to push herself standing, sliding up and onto her feet. The man climbs the stairs after her. Kylie hops forward once, bumps her shoulder against the open door so that it closes just as he's halfway up.

Her final glimpse into the basement is of him, his wide-eyed, wet-mouthed, disbelieving face. Then the door is solidly shut. She turns her back against it, stands on tiptoe to reach the knob with her bound hands, fumbles the lock in her fingers, gives it a twist. The basement door violently shakes as her captor throws his body against the other side. The doorknob rattles in her grasp. But it's no use.

She's already locked him in.

TWENTY-ONE

BARBARA

I SET my phone down on the steps beside me. I take another sip of wine, even though I should probably begin winding down now. I've already drank two-thirds of the bottle. I eye the plate on the ground at the bottom of the steps and I'm struck with disappointment that I didn't get to try a single cookie or brownie. There might still be one intact, though if there is it's in the dirt now. Not to mention, I'm not sure I want to eat anything that was remotely close to that raccoon's filthy paws.

Are raccoon paws filthy? I have no idea.

The sky grumbles with thunder. Far across the lake, the distant horizon flashes and blooms with more lightning still. I crane my neck toward the branches over the clearing, surprised I still haven't seen a drop of rain. Probably later in the night I'll hear it, after I wake up covered in sweat like I usually do. The wine certainly won't help in that regard, when my body decides to process all the sugar and alcohol at 3 AM. Maybe I'm fortunate then, that I didn't wolf down a bunch of baked goods on top of the rest...

The sky erupts with the loudest *bang* of thunder I've heard yet, startling me. The lightning must have been close that time. After the initial fright, I catch myself smiling. I do love a good thunder storm.

I check my phone again to see if Hank has replied to my story about the raccoon. Not yet. He's probably zoned in on whatever movie he's watching tonight, with his own pizza and snacks and beer. I wouldn't mind joining him for a night like that, either.

I set my phone down, stand up, and carefully make my way to the bottom of the porch steps, where I stretch my hands over my head and groan pleasantly. At the precise moment I do, another whip-crack of thunder sends me stiffening in place. I even scream a little. My heart pounds. I can't help but laugh at myself. Then I hear what sounds like the gentle pitter-patter of rain beginning to fall. Very light, caught in the leaves and branches overhead.

The storm lures me onward. I traipse across the clearing toward the lake dock. The clouds illuminate white and blue with lightning. Between the louder claps of thunder, a constant low growl moves through the sky. I stop at the beginning of the dock. The water ripples with droplets. The sound of the thunder and the delicate rain is so incredibly soothing to my drunk mind, I find myself swaying a bit. I inhale deeply, tasting the fresh rain as much as smelling it.

God, I'm buzzed.

Thunder takes me by surprise yet again, as powerful and near as before. Perhaps I shouldn't stand in the open like I am, though I'm sure a tree would be struck before me. Can't say that for certain, though.

Feeling I've tempted mother nature enough, I reluctantly move away from the dock, before turning on my heel and starting for the house again.

Oh, how I wish Hank was here. The only thing that would make this whole evening even better would be his arms wrapped around me. Just the thought of it fills me with—

Halfway to the porch, another noise steals my attention. Something beneath the rolling thunder and rain and whispering leaves. A feverish, high-pitched *squeal,* followed by a swift series of bleats. Instantly upsetting. I stop dead in my tracks, turn my head in its direction, and find myself looking at my car parked a short distance from the porch, from me. Thunder quakes again and the sound is lost. I approach its general direction. My car. As the thunder dissipates, the sound reemerges. It's a creature's *mewling.* Something in pain. The closer I get to my car, the better I can hear it, and the sound sends an awful, sobering shiver up my spine. At the hood of my car, I crouch down, peering underneath. Something's there. A dark shape. An animal. It's too dark to see.

After a brief hesitation, I jump to my feet and hurry back to the house, climbing the porch steps with a slight clumsiness about me, using the railing for assistance. I head inside, quickening my pace to the kitchen counter where I snatch up my flashlight. I return outside with it. Lightning flashes, showering the clearing in its harsh white-blue. Thunder claps shortly after.

Back to my car, I drop to the dirt on my hands and knees. I lower myself further down onto the ground and shine my flashlight's bright beam beneath my car's under-carriage.

"Oh God."

Beside the rear passenger tire, the raccoon lays on its side, its body hiccuping violently, a slow gush of foam leaking from its snarling mouth.

TWENTY-TWO

KYLIE

Kylie nearly screams with relief, in triumph.

But she's not free yet.

"Oh my God, oh my God," she mutters as she jumps steadily through the dark, ping-ponging from one side of the hallway to the other.

Behind her, the man pounds on the door. He shouts something, but his voice is too weak and muffled to understand. Kylie pays him no mind.

At the end of the hallway, she emerges into a small but beautifully decorated kitchen. Tidy. It's awkward and slow, but she leans with her back against the kitchen counter and opens the first drawer she comes to. Kitchen towels. Useless. Across from her, on the other countertop, she spots a cutlery block. Unfortunately, it's placed near the wall and, with her hands tied behind her back, she can already hardly reach a thing.

"If you actually think you're getting away, you'd better... you'd better think..."

The man shouts through the door, but seems unable to complete his thought. Kylie ignores him.

She opens another drawer. This one is full of random odds and ends. A pen, a notepad, a vegetable peeler, an ice cream scoop, a six-inch ruler, a pair of scissors, a melon baller, a—

A pair of scissors.

Kylie stuffs her hands into the drawer and manages to separate the scissors from the rest of the junk. She's trembling. With fear, with desperation, with hope. She pries the scissors open. She fiddles with them, struggling to get the twine between the blades without stabbing herself in the wrist.

The scissors slip from her grasp and clatter to the floor.

"Damn it."

Down the hallway, the man pounds against the door. He pounds harder than before. Is he kicking it now, she wonders? The thumps and bangs seem to reverberate through the whole house.

Kylie drops to the floor, scrabbles the scissors back into her hands. She stays there, her bound legs folded beneath herself as she lifts her face to the ceiling in concentration, blindly working the scissors behind her back. She manages to slip one of the blades under the twine. She squeezes the handles shut. The scissors seem to snag. Not the sharpest tool in the drawer, apparently…

"Please. Please, for the love of God."

She opens the scissors again. She has to really *pull* the blades open, as the twine is somehow jammed between them. Once she gets them apart, she closes the blades slightly, repositions them so they're not at an angle to the twine, and gently closes them the rest of the way. Delicate. Precise. She feels the vibration through the scissors' handles as the twine begins to split between the blades. With one last, audible *snip*, the binds around her wrists fall loose. She presents her own hands before herself like she's never seen such appendages before.

Down the hall, the man gives the door another hefty kick. Kylie hears what sounds like splintering wood.

She makes quick work of the twine around her ankles.

She's free. She's *actually* free.

Not quite. Not yet.

She jumps upright. She ditches the scissors on the kitchen counter, pulls a knife from the cutlery block. A serrated steak knife. She scans the rest of the countertop, the surrounding kitchen, hoping for anything else that might help her. Car keys? Surely his car is parked outside, or perhaps in his garage.

With another kick, the basement door flies open, rockets against the wall behind it. Kylie flinches so badly she nearly screams. The man tumbles through, falling drunkenly against the wall opposite the door. He crumbles to his knees there. He fights to get standing. Whatever's wrong with him, whatever he's battling with inside, it appears he's still sick with it. Knife still in hand, he pushes away from the wall, swaying to his feet.

Kylie can't afford to waste another second. She bolts out of the kitchen, races for the next door she sees—what she assumes must be the front door, which she's heard open and shut so many times already from down below. She yanks it open, stumbles across its threshold into the breezy, stormy night beyond.

Darkness. Dirt. Trees. *Nature.*

Behind her, the man lets loose howling in pursuit.

She darts down a handful of porch steps, past the small pickup truck parked there, and is promptly faced with an immense body of water before her, choked on all sides by lush forest trees. Lightning daggers the churning clouds above. A percussion of thunder rattles her where she stands.

"Hey!" her captor screams from the porch.

She can't simply keep running. He'll catch her easily enough. Her little steak knife will hardly save her, either, she thinks.

Only one thing is for certain: she's not letting him take her back.

Heavy footsteps gaining at her heels, she runs straight for the little dock over the water. Her bare feet slap the dirt, the wooden planks, thumping hard in quick succession until the end of the dock draws near, the black water beyond it.

Kylie jumps.

She hits the water elegantly enough. It splashes over her in a surge of cold, blinding darkness. She opens her eyes, submerged, as the depths flicker to life with lightning on the water's surface. But it isn't life she sees down below. In the fraction of an electric moment, Kylie glimpses a collection of long, slender rolls of weighted tarp along the lake bottom, strands of billowing hair creeping out from their ends. She recoils from the sight, swims for the surface. She resurfaces gasping, the stormy air wonderful in her lungs. She treads water for a moment, disoriented.

"God, fucking, dammit!"

She turns to the barking voice and sees him at the end of the dock. He's fallen to his knees there, is struggling to pick himself up. He's not getting in the water, though. She's escaped him. For now.

Lightning flashes again. Thunder massages the storm clouds from one horizon to the next. Staying afloat, Kylie swivels in the water, assessing her options, and her eyes immediately fasten to the *other* lights across the lake. Another cabin there. Someone else. Someone who *isn't* this man. Someone who might help her, she thinks. *Prays.*

She lets go of the knife in her hand, lets it sink below. Easier to swim without it, she thinks, without worrying that she'll stab herself in the process.

Buoyed with hope, Kylie swims for rescue.

PART TWO
NIGHT TERRORS

TWENTY-THREE

BARBARA

I'M TEMPORARILY FROZEN, my flashlight aimed on the dying creature beneath my car. All thought vacates my mind. There are dots to be connected here, I know there are, but at the moment I'm incapable of drawing the lines. I'm incapable of moving. I'm lucky my heart beats on its own, or I'd probably fall over dead my head is so *blank.*

The raccoon shivers and whines in its final death throes. Then all at once it goes still. Silent.

The first thought that pieces itself together is this: *Is chocolate deadly for raccoons? Like dogs?*

Whatever my second thought might be, it's interrupted as someone's scream pierces the night.

"Help!"

I jolt up off the ground like a coiled spring, onto my knees, jerking toward the sound, toward the voice, sweeping my flashlight across the trees and toward the water where a body crawls out, panting and spluttering and sopping wet.

"Please," the girl rasps. *"Help me…"*

I'm stunned once again, unable to make sense of anything that's happening at the moment, but my mind kicks into action much faster than before anyhow. Call it instinct, a reflex. I jump to my feet and hurry to her, *run* to her, the beam from my flashlight bouncing wildly across the dirt before me. The girl barely picks herself up. Her entire body heaves with exhaustion. As I aim my light on her, I immediately notice the bruises on her arms, her throat. Her shirt, clinging wetly to her small frame, is stained with blood from her shoulder.

She peers directly into my eyes, lashes dripping, and says, "I need help…"

"What's happened to you?" I take her gently by the arms. "Where did you come from…"

I peer toward the lake itself, as thunder crashes over our heads.

"He's coming," she says, and a wave of chills breaks over me, so strong I viscerally shiver with them. "He's coming for me…"

"Who's coming?"

I look past her once more, my eyes skipping like a stone across the lake water toward the nearest property in sight. The *only* property in sight. Sterling's property.

Is it possible, I wonder? She could have come from anywhere, really, someplace even farther than that. Hell, I'm sure there are numerous other properties surrounding this lake I can't see from this vantage point, nestled into the trees just like mine—like Cassidy's, I mean.

I suppose it doesn't matter. This girl needs help. *Now.*

Before she can answer my question, we're each distracted by the sudden arrival of *headlights* through the nearby trees—a vehicle making its way along the twisting driveway toward Cassidy's lake house, toward us. My heart leaps at the sight of it. Is it *him?* Her captor, coming to reclaim her? The car comes around the bend, rolling slowly. As soon as it enters the clearing, I recognize it.

"Shit," the girl says. "It's them."

"Hey, wait…" I can hardly spit out my words as she grabs me by the hand and pulls me frantically toward the house. Her grip tightens on me, as my clumsy feet trip over themselves, struggling to keep up with her quickening pace. "That's not him. That's…"

Hold on—did she say *them?*

We're already to the porch steps. It takes all my concentration not to stumble and fall flat on my face. Behind us, Cassidy's headlights sweep the front of the house, throwing our shadows across the porch as the girl practically drags me through the entrance and inside. She slams the door behind us, twists the lock.

"Wait a second," I tell her again. "That's not him. That's my friend, Cassidy. She's… well, a friend from work. She's letting me stay here."

The girl faces me, her youthful features drawn with so much worry. Her eyes dart around us, this *place,* as if some terrible realization has come over her. Then she breaks away from me. She spots the light switch by the door and flips everything down, dropping the house into complete darkness. Well, almost complete. I'm still holding the flashlight, which she grabs right from my hand and flips it off as well, then hands it back to me rather forcefully.

She goes to the window and pulls the drapes aside, peering out. I'm still reeling from everything—the dying raccoon, this obviously traumatized young woman climbing out of the lake screaming for help. I decide to indulge her, joining her at the window. I'm fairly certain Cassidy must have already seen us racing across the clearing and into the house. At the very least, she saw the lights go out.

"You said *them*," I whisper to the girl, as we watch Cassidy's car pull up next to mine. "Is there more than one person after you?"

"That's the car," she says with confidence, staring unblinkingly at the vehicle in question.

The headlights are almost shining right on us, slightly off the window toward the front door. The driver's door opens. A figure emerges, obscured behind the bright lights, but I can already tell it's Cassidy. Because I'm so flustered with everything else going on, I barely possess the head-space to wonder what the hell she's even doing here again, as if her first unexpected visit wasn't enough.

"That's her," the girl says.

Two words, and my stomach plummets into ice.

"What do you mean, that's her," I repeat listlessly.

"She stopped for me," the girl goes on. Her eyes are fixed on the figure still standing by the open car door. "She asked if I was all right, then asked if I needed a ride. I said yes. I got into the car and..." The girl swallows down her fear, or whatever emotion she's grappling with. "...I didn't know he was in the backseat."

Another wave of chills races across my shoulders, up my back, lifting the hairs on the nape of my neck. The figure outside leaves the car running, leaves the door open, as it steps around and moves into the headlights, from a shadow in the dark to a silhouette in the light. But it's Cassidy all right. My head feels like it's spinning on my shoulders around and around, dizzy and sick, and this time it isn't the wine.

"She helped him take me," the girl finishes.

We both watch as Cassidy climbs the porch steps. She seems to notice something at the top, at her feet. She crouches and picks it up. My already sinking heart plunges coldly down into whatever depths my stomach disappeared to. Cassidy stands straight, my phone in her hands. We ran right past it on our way in. I didn't even stop to think...

"Barbara?" Cassidy calls out, looking from my phone to the door. *"Barbara, you in there?"*

She steps closer to the door where we can no longer see her. The girl and I both turn to see the knob as Cassidy tries it from the other side.

"Barbara?"

Is this really happening? I'm almost tempted to pinch myself.

Next to me, the girl gasps. I follow her gaze outside, across the clearing, beyond Cassidy's car. A second pair of headlights appears through the trees, pulling into the clearing. A small pickup truck. It parks behind Cassidy's vehicle. The lights shut off. Someone climbs out. A man. I can't tell for certain, but my gut already warns me who it will be— who I *know* it must be. The man steps into the headlights. Some part of me wants to unlock the door and let Cassidy inside, or better yet scream for her to run. But then she steps into view, away from the door at the head of the porch steps.

"Daddy? What are you doing here?"

My already fractured mind crumbles in on itself. I exchange a glance with the girl. She must see the absolute bewilderment on my face as she raises her own brow, as if to say *I told you so.*

Daddy? I think. *Really?*

He takes another step into the headlights. His handsome salt-and-pepper face might as well be clear as day. It's Sterling, no doubt about it. Cassidy descends the creaking porch steps toward him. Every fiber of my being is urging me to move now, to escape this place. But I'm rooted to the spot. I watch Cassidy greet Sterling, each of them standing blocked in shadow against the bright headlights, gesturing toward the house, then pointing toward the house across the lake in kind.

"They know I'm here," the girl murmurs beside me.

My heart is beating a thousand times per second. I still can't believe this is happening. Who is this girl? Who is Sterling? Who the hell is Cassidy, really?

Why did she invite me to this place?

Cassidy leaves her father, returns to her open car door. She leans inside and suddenly the headlights fall dark. Everything falls dark, except the flicker of lightning out over the lake. When Cassidy stands straight again and shuts her car door, I see she's got something in her hand. Something besides her keys, which I'm certain she'll soon use to let herself inside. She approaches the house once again, raising the object until it's pointed skyward.

"Shit," the girl says, stealing the words right off the tip of my tongue. "She's got a gun."

TWENTY-FOUR

KYLIE

THE WOMAN OUTSIDE—APPARENTLY her name is Cassidy—gestures to the man behind her—apparently her father. She makes a circular motion with her hand, what Kylie understands to be a suggestion of circling the property. Her father obeys and begins making his way around, disappearing into the shadows.

"Are there any other doors open?" Kylie asks. "Or windows?"

"Just the windows upstairs," the woman beside her replies.

Barbara, Kylie reminds herself. Or at least that's the name the woman outside called through the door.

The woman climbs the porch steps again, this time wielding a pistol which she keeps raised alongside her face as she comes, like she's watched one too many police procedurals. She approaches the door again where they can't see her.

"Barbara? It's me, Cassidy. I have your phone. Is everything

all right?"

It sounds like genuine concern, except for the mention of Barbara's phone. Somehow that sounds like a warning. *I have your phone, so don't bother trying to call for help.*

"I'm letting myself in now, all right?"

In that same instant, Barbara takes Kylie by the hand and pulls her away from the window, away from the door. They flee through the house on bare feet, both of them. Barbara pulls Kylie up the stairs toward what appears to be an open loft. There's *another* set of stairs there. Except it's not stairs, Kylie realizes. It's a ladder coming down from what must be the attic. Kylie vaguely wonders why the attic ladder is already pulled down for them this way.

Barbara grabs something up off the floor—a hook puller, for opening the attic door. She tosses it up through the attic opening.

"Hurry," she tells Kylie, and nods to the ladder.

Kylie doesn't need to be told twice. She's halfway up the ladder when she hears the door downstairs open. She climbs into the dark, musty attic as quietly as possible. She winces as Barbara follows behind, also as quietly as possible but still making some amount of noise. Kylie prays the woman downstairs doesn't hear them. She moves aside to make room for Barbara as she climbs up beside her. Then, appearing to hold her breath, Barbara reaches down and begins pulling the ladder up. It makes a little bit of noise. Metallic rattling. Kylie is almost certain the woman downstairs will hear it. Then the ladder is in the attic with them, the attic door shut. Kylie and Barbara both pause and listen. Kylie meets Barbara's eyes as they do, each of their mouths parted as they try to slow their shallow breaths.

Down below, very faintly, *"Barbara?"*

Kylie takes a deep but silent breath, willing her nerves to calm. She can't believe how close to freedom she was, how close to safety, to escape. She can't believe how close her captor still is, so close to discovering her again, so close to being right back where she started.

"Now what?" she whispers.

The woman, Barbara, turns to her with a look in her eyes, like she hasn't thought much farther ahead than this. She has to think about it for a moment. She peers across the dark attic, toward something on the other side.

"That vent is open," she whispers. Kylie follows her gaze and sees it, a sizable vent door that's open on its hinges, leading outside. "We can get out that way if we have to…"

Kylie looks around the attic, then eyes the attic door itself. "What are we waiting for?"

"They'll hear us," Barbara says. "We need to wait."

Even in the near complete darkness, there's a sweaty sheen along the contour of Barbara's face. She stares at the attic door with a distracted look about her, her mind far away. Kylie imagines this must be the last thing she expected to happen to her tonight. How confused she must have been when Kylie first climbed out of the lake, calling for help…

"I'm up here, daddy!"

Down below, Cassidy's voice is so abrupt and *near* that Kylie almost flinches. She must be in the loft. Too close to the attic door, Kylie fears. She holds her breath, listening as Cassidy is joined by her father. Their voices murmur a bit, audible but not understandable, until their footsteps draw near, thumping steadily until it sounds as though they're directly beneath the attic door itself. Kylie tenses. Hunched on all fours, she feels on the brink of falling over, overcome with the urge to move, or helplessly fidget in some way, giving away their hiding place. She concentrates all her efforts on staying perfectly still.

"I checked all around the house and nothing," the man says.

"Shit," his daughter replies. *"Maybe they took off out the back door after I pulled up."*

"The back door is locked. I don't think they left that way."

"Then where the hell are they?"

The voices in the loft fall silent, and all at once Kylie is one-hundred-percent certain their would-be captors are eying the underside of the attic door.

She exchanges another look with the woman beside her. Barbara swallows down her own nerves, making a loud *gulp* sound as she does. If she's struggling to hold still like Kylie is, Kylie understands her plight completely. She feels her body shivering, her arms and legs aching, perched on them like she is, willing herself not to move an inch. Her swim across the lake already exhausted her. She's not sure she can hold this position for long, on her hands and knees.

Slowly, silently, with her legs folded under herself Kylie rests her haunches onto her heels, easing her weight off her trembling arms.

"A couple windows are open up here," the man says. *"Think they could have gone out that way?"*

"*I think they're still inside,*" Cassidy says. "*We need to search everything.*"

"*But if they* did *go out one of the windows, they could be getting away right now.*"

"*I don't think Barbara climbed out one of the windows, dad,*" Cassidy says matter-of-factly. "*She's too old.*"

Ouch, Kylie thinks. The way Barbara grimaces in the dark, Kylie's pretty sure the comment smarted.

"*She's not that old, Cass,*" the man says. "*I spoke to her myself.*"

"*Yeah, well, congratulations on that,*" Cassidy snaps. Even without seeing their faces, Kylie can practically hear their prickly expressions. "*Why the hell did you have to get involved, anyway? I asked you to stay out of it.*"

"*All I did was say hello to the woman. I'd hardly call that getting involved.*"

"*You did a lot more than say hello...*"

"*How was I supposed to know those cookies were yours? Or that you were trying to drug the woman? I thought your plan was to come in the middle of the—*"

"*My plan was to handle this on my own, like I said. I told you to stay out of it. I thought that was enough.*"

"*You would have needed my help eventually.*"

"*Yes, but I had the rest covered. I didn't need you sniffing around.*" Cassidy lets out a gruff, irritated growl. "*Anyway, it's too late for that. We need to search every inch of this place...*"

Kylie and Barbara sit still as statues as they listen to the others begin scouring the house below. Kylie's wound so tight she feels a soreness in her neck and shoulders. She allows herself to loosen up a bit, now the others are no longer right underneath them. She wonders how long they'll be waiting up here. Until morning? Is there any chance the two downstairs *don't* include the attic in their search?

Kylie isn't sure she can handle the suspense, but for now, she has no choice.

TWENTY-FIVE

BARBARA

I COULD ALMOST FEEL the alcohol in my bloodstream evaporate at the sight of Cassidy's gun. Whatever buzz I still had from my wine drinking is entirely gone. Not only am I sober, but my senses feel exaggerated, heightened, in a state of hyper focus.

I discreetly watch the girl beside me while we wait. It's impossible not to notice her age, or what I assume her age must be. She's a high schooler, I think. So young. *Too* young. Sixteen, seventeen, perhaps? I'm tempted to ask her name as we wait with bated breath, but I know now's not the time. I feel silly for even being tempted to initiate conversation at a time like this. Perhaps it must be some innate part of me coming out, I think, some parental need. An urge I have to squash for now. There is another need that surfaces alongside it, one I feel incapable of resisting— and that's the need to keep this girl safe from the monsters downstairs. There's no debate in my mind. I saw the bruises around her throat, the bloodstain on her shirt. She's been through some kind of hell already. She's fought to make it this far.

I'm not letting them have her again.

We sit in such utter silence, such utter *stillness,* that I get a cramp in my foot. It's out of my control, and yet as it comes on—as inevitable as a hot flash—I clench my jaw in annoyance with myself, like *of course* I'd get a cramp in my foot right now, at the worst possible time. I grin and bear it. Except that's a lie, I'm not grinning at all.

I'm about to reposition my foot when Sterling's voice suddenly speaks out below us and I hold very still instead, the cramping pain nearly unbearable.

"Hey, Cuss? Where's the hook puller?"

From someplace farther away downstairs, Cassidy calls out, *"What?"*

"Where's the hook puller? You know, for the attic!"

Shit.

Shit, shit, shit.

I meet the girl's gaze next to me, both of us thinking the same thing.

Shit.

"What do you need the hook puller for?" Cassidy says, joining her father. *"You really think they could be up there?"*

"We've searched everywhere else. If they're not up there, then they're outside. And if they're outside, we've given them a damned good head start—"

"Yeah, yeah," Cassidy interrupts. *"It's around here some-where. I haven't been up there in a while."*

The girl looks at me with a wide-eyed stare, as if to say *'okay, now what?'* We're definitely cornered up here. There *is* the open vent, which I consider a last resort. Our *only* resort, really, should Cassidy and Sterling come up here. The girl can probably make it out just fine. I'm not so sure about myself. Should we take that route, we'll be climbing around on the roof. Where to go from there, I have no idea. Despite resenting Cassidy's earlier remark—*she's too old*—I can't help realizing she's right. I'm too old to be jumping off rooftops. I'm not a springy young *thing* like the girl beside me.

"*Hold on,*" Sterling says down below. "*I'm getting something to stand on.*"

"Damn it," I whisper aloud. "Come on, let's go."

I crawl first, leading the way across the dusty attic floor, dodging dust bunnies and rat droppings alike. Our knees knock and bump the floor the whole way. I wince at each noise we make, knowing full well the others must hear it. They *know* we're up here now.

To confirm my fears, Cassidy's voice calls out loud and clear, "*I hear 'em, daddy! They're up there! They're up there!*"

I reach the vent, crouched at its opening on my hands and knees. It's a sizable drop down to the patio roof. A bad landing could easily spill an unbalanced person right over the roof's edge to the ground below.

Long story short, I don't think I can make it.

"Come on," I say. "You first."

Behind us, the attic door pulls open. The metallic ladder bangs and rattles down into the loft. The girl takes a look through the gable vent herself. I can see it in her eyes, the drop isn't easy for either of us.

"Are you gonna be able to do this?" she asks.

I'm touched by her concern, despite our circumstances.

"Can *you* make it?" I ask her.

She peers down to the roof below. "Yeah, I can make it."

"Then go. Quickly. But be careful about it."

Hurry, but be careful about it. Talk about mixed signals.

The girl dangles her legs to start. Then she delicately turns herself around in the vent's opening, supporting herself with her upper body alone as she lowers herself out. I reach for her, my hands hovering worriedly. She's breathing hard. She's shaking. For a moment I fear this whole idea is a mistake, that she'll fall and break her neck. My instinct is to grab her, haul her back into the attic beside me. Then she lets go. She drops. So does my stomach.

I hear her land. A rough thump. I stick my head outside, my eyes gaping as wide as my mouth. She only slips slightly where she lands, throws her hands out to catch herself against the house's siding. She cranes her neck to see me above her. Anticipating. Expectant.

Before she can say a word I tell her to run.

TWENTY-SIX

KYLIE

THE WOMAN, Barbara, tells her to run before vanishing back inside the attic, and all Kylie wants to do is scream *'Where?'*

She understands Barbara can't follow. But Kylie is aimless and knows it. She looks around herself, at the surrounding trees, at the ten-foot drop to the ground below. She feels the lightest sprinkle of rain from the storm clouds overhead.

Behind her, something rattles onto the shingled roof. She turns and sees it—the screen from one of the upstairs windows, pushed out by her captor. He emerges there, clambering out one leg at a time.

With nowhere to go but down, Kylie goes to the roof's edge. She sits, dangles her legs over, and like before lowers herself down from the ledge. The man's footsteps hammer the roof, thumping madly in her direction. She glimpses him drawing upon her, a dark hulking shadow in the storm. She lets go.

The drop is fast, but it feels like she's suspended for

ages, her belly quivering with the fall. Her feet hit the dirt. She allows herself to fold, rolling back onto her butt, her back. She lays there for a moment, scattered and jarred from the impact. The man leans over the edge of the roof, peering down, once again unable to follow.

Kylie picks herself up. Standing between the property and the woods, she peers toward the clearing, the lake beyond. Then she peers into the trees, the darkness within them. Lightning strobes in the sky, fragmenting the woods into pillars of light and dark. With nowhere else to go, she bolts into the trees.

The dirt is hard but cool on the undersides of her feet. She runs aimlessly, dodging through the easiest gaps in the trees, over exposed roots, going as fast as she can, blind as can be. She chances a glance over her shoulder and sees nothing. No one in pursuit. Not yet, anyway.

Where am I going? she thinks.

What will become of Barbara, whom she's left behind?

Kylie can't think about that right now. Truth be told, she's not entirely concerned about Barbara. She hasn't the bandwidth to worry about such things, to worry outside herself at this moment. She runs hard, panting and gasping. Even after swimming across the lake, she's still somehow got energy to burn, a second wind, perhaps. Maybe it's adrenaline—her sheer will to survive, wherever the hell *that* came from.

She keeps going, with nothing but the night and the intermittent flash of lightning to show her the way.

TWENTY-SEVEN

BARBARA

"Stop!" Cassidy screams from behind me. "Not one more move or I'll shoot!"

She's standing on the ladder, halfway inside the attic, her pistol held in both hands and trained on my back. I don't doubt her ability to shoot me here on the spot. And seeing as I'm fairly certain the drop from the gable vent will paralyze me, I do as she says.

"Come over here," Cassidy orders. "Now."

After a deep breath, I begin crawling back to the attic door, closer and closer to the muzzle of that gun in Cassidy's hands. A deadly black eye. Does she *really* know what she's doing with that thing? As I crawl my way toward her, tonight's revelations gradually come back to me, one after another—Sterling's little visits, Cassidy's earlier visit to drop off her homemade treats, the raccoon which suffered an agonizing death thanks to said treats, inadvertently saving my life…

Cassidy invited me here with the intention of poisoning me.

"What is this, Cassidy?" I ask, halfway across the dark attic. "Why are you doing this?"

"Let's save the chit chat for another time," she says. "Just keep coming. Nice and easy."

She takes a couple precarious steps down the ladder, holding the top rung with one hand, her gun in the other, making room for me to climb down after her. I crawl to the mouth of the attic door, peering down. Her gun is still trained on me, on my face. I can feel it—being one wrong move from death, one little accidental twitch of Cassidy's finger from *lights out.* She steps further down the ladder, then steps onto solid ground below. As soon as she lets off the ladder, she takes the gun in both hands again, but in the instant before she does I see the gun trembling like crazy.

They've got the lights on again, both in the loft and downstairs below, and I can see the wild fear reflected in Cassidy's eyes. This whole situation is outside of her wheelhouse. Probably why she preferred poisoning me over something simpler like a gun to the head. I have to remind myself, however, that she's unpredictable. I can't trust my own assumptions here. If push comes to shove, I'm sure she'll shoot.

Down below, somewhere I can't see him, Sterling calls out, *"She's gone into the damned woods!"*

Cassidy glances his way, briefly, keeping her eyes mostly trained on me.

"Okay, well, I've got this under control if you wanna go after her," she tells her father.

"The hell you do," Sterling says, coming to stand beside her as I'm lowering myself onto the ladder, following like an obedient little lamb. "Goddammit, Cass, this whole thing is a mess..."

"I said I have it under control, daddy."

Daddy. Something about the way Cassidy says it grates on me, makes me grimace with my back to them, carefully lowering myself down one rung at a time.

"I wouldn't describe any of this as being *'under control.'*"

"Would you *stop*?" Cassidy groans. "Go and get her already. I've got this one. Please."

I reach the bottom of the ladder, step off the final rung to face them. Cassidy's got her gun trained on me just a few steps away. Her father, Sterling, stands just over her shoulder, eyeing me with contempt, his eyes flashing between me and his daughter. He doesn't trust her abilities in the slightest. Judging by what I know of Cassidy's work ethic, he's probably right not to.

"I don't need your help," she says. Her eyes flicker toward him, where she surely feels him breathing down her neck. "The longer you stay here... *hovering* over me... the farther that girl's going to get..."

With one final irritated growl, Sterling turns on his heel and rushes down the loft stairs. I listen for his footsteps as he leaves, out the front door and onto the porch and finally out of earshot.

"You're going to do as I say," Cassidy tells me. "Because you don't want to bite the bullet, so to speak, right?"

I want to mock her so badly. I want to ask if she came up with that all on her own. I want to ask if she's ever really handled a gun before. If she's ever done *anything like this* before. I truly can't imagine sweet, polite, *there-are-donuts-*

in-the-break-room Cassidy doing something like this. Even seeing her now, with my own eyes, it's unbelievable. But then I think: perhaps the simple fact that this seems so *unlike her* is a testament to how well she's pulled the wool over all our eyes.

She steps aside, giving me a clear path from the attic ladder toward the head of the loft stairs.

"Walk," she says. "Nice and easy. Downstairs. I'll be right behind you."

I do as she says. I walk with my hands at my sides, slowly but surely. I pause at the top of the stairs.

"Do you know who that girl is?" I ask. "That your father's been holding onto?"

"Downstairs," she repeats, ignoring my question. "Now."

I oblige. I take the stairs one at a time, nice and easy, just like she told me.

"That girl, she told me... she told me you helped your father take her. Is that true?"

"That's none of your business."

Her feet whisper on the steps behind me. Her hands must be sweaty, slippery, because I hear her adjust her grip on the gun. She might be slightly out of her element, but there's a danger in that as well. She could be clumsy. She could be rash. I reach the bottom of the stairs and pause with no further instruction.

"Why are you doing this?" I ask her again.

"Over there," she orders.

I have to look back to see her, to see where exactly she wants me to go. She nods toward the kitchen. I look that way myself. There's nothing over there I can see, nowhere to go… except for the locked door in the corner. Is that where I'm headed? If that's her plan, I'm curious why she didn't allow her father to help escort me down there. She was so eager to send him away, to do this on her own, like a child with something to prove.

"Come on now," she says. "We don't have all day…"

Just as she says this, just as I take my next step, a familiar, electronic tune begins to play. A melodic series of chirps. It's familiar to me because it's *mine*. It's my phone, my husband's ringtone, ringing in Cassidy's pocket. I can't resist glancing over my shoulder at the sound, surprised to hear it. Cassidy's surprised as well. While her hands remain on the gun, and the gun remains pointed between my shoulder blades, her head is down, eyeing herself, confused by the abrupt jingle coming from her back pocket.

It's now or never.

I turn on my heel, swipe my arm against Cassidy's wrists, knocking her hands and the gun therein aside. I wince a little, expecting the gun to fire, for Cassidy's itchy trigger finger to pull, but it doesn't. I step into her, grab her wrist in one hand, her throat in the other. I jerk her arm skyward, getting the muzzle of her pistol as far from myself as possible as I barge against her, send her staggering backward, both our feet shuffling and scraping. My phone continues to ring in her back pocket. Cassidy snarls. Spittle specks my face from her bared teeth. She kicks at me and I return the favor. I drive her backward, toward the stairs we just descended from. The backs of her ankles meet the bottom step and she goes down. I crumple on top of her. I can't help it. We each land on the staircase. The gun drops from Cassidy's grasp, goes skipping across the floor into the shadows toward the back bedroom behind the stairs. I reach around her, groping and scrabbling for my phone sticking out of her back pocket. I pinch it between my fingers. She grabs at me likewise, tries to throw me off. She partially succeeds, except I've still got a hold on her and we both spill off the side of the stairs and onto the hard floor in a grunting heap. The landing knocks the wind out of me.

My phone falls out of Cassidy's pocket, face up, my husband's name illuminated on the screen.

I reach for it. Cassidy bats it away, sends it spiraling across the floor toward the living room sofa. Lying on my side, I plant my foot into Cassidy's gut and force her off me. She tumbles back with a breathless sound: *Ack!*

I scurry after my phone on all fours. I reach for it, hunched with my hair in my face, in my mouth. Cassidy is moving behind me. I drag my finger across the little bubble, answering the call. I open my mouth to speak, to shout my husband's name, as the underside of Cassidy's boot strikes me square in the side of the head. I collapse onto my side. My vision immediately swims with stars. I blink my eyes in a daze, my mouth still open, stunned, my phone still held loosely in my hand.

"Hank," I say. It comes out of me like a whisper.

Cassidy kicks the phone from my grasp. I roll over, my brain pounding, and watch as she follows it rattling across the floor. I find my voice and I scream.

"Hank! I need help!"

With an angry grunt, Cassidy stomps my phone under

the heel of her boot and the screen cracks. She stomps it again, and again and again, until the screen is dark and surrounded with pieces of broken glass and plastic. Once my phone is good and dead, she turns on me, panting heavily, her eyes staring daggers into mine.

"You stupid *bitch*," she says.

She rushes past me, toward the other side of the room. I push myself up onto my hands and knees. I'm shaking. I feel sick. I lift my gaze just as she returns, just in time to receive a cold, jarring lash across my temple with the barrel of her gun. The stars in my vision swim up again, swirling like the particles of a snow globe.

Cassidy moves away for a moment. If I were quicker, more resilient, more athletic, I might jump to my feet and run in the time she's busying herself with something else across the room. But instead I'm stuck trying to hold myself up as my own blood trickles onto the floor before my very eyes.

I hear the jingle of keys. The opening of a door. Cassidy returns to me. She's all stomping feet and noisy nostrils. She grabs me by the hair, a fistful from the back of my head, and urges me in the direction of the kitchen once more.

"Get up," she demands. Her voice is pitching all over the place with nerves. "Come on, Barbara, get up."

She must have really walloped me with her gun, because I feel a stream of warm blood spill off the shelf of my jaw, down my neck as I clamber to my feet. She keeps hold of my hair, jabs her gun into the small of my back, and pushes me ahead.

"*Move.*"

She directs me into the kitchen, toward the door that's now standing wide open. It's not a pantry or a closet like I first guessed, but a set of stairs leading into the basement.

"Cassidy," I say. "Please…"

I barely reach the head of the stairs when she shoves me forward. I stumble into the waiting dark, my arms open wide to catch myself. Except there's nothing to catch myself on. I soar into it, into the nothing, flying for all of two seconds before hitting the stairs *hard,* and tumbling down them like a sack of rocks. I spill to the floor at the bottom, roll to a stop on what feels like cold cement. Every inch of me aches. I'm lucky I didn't break anything. Or maybe I did, and I just don't know it yet…

I peer back up the stairs where Cassidy stands like a faceless specter looking down at me in my bruised, pitiful state.

Without another word, she slams the door shut.

The lock clicks back into place.

TWENTY-EIGHT

KYLIE

SHE'S STILL JOGGING STEADILY AHEAD when she steals a peek at the woods behind her and spots him. Not him, exactly, but the flashlight he carries. Its bright beam cutting through the trees. Then it turns off. Kylie slows. Lightning flashes, splashing the woods with wild shadows. One of those shadows in the distance continues moving in her direction. It's him. He's deliberately turned off his flashlight, but he's still coming. Has he spotted her, she wonders? Does he hope to get the jump on her?

The flashlight comes back on. It sweeps the trees, aims downward at the ground for a moment, then turns off once more. It's then Kylie realizes what he's doing. She eyes the ground for herself. With another spark of lightning, she sees her own footprints in the dirt, deep enough, defined enough, to easily make out with a bit of light.

He'll have no problem tracking her this way.

She studies the ground around herself. The woods are smattered with patches of underbrush, with fallen sticks and branches. Without any time to lose, she takes a wide, careful step onto such a branch beside her. She lunges off that branch and into a patch of wild grass, flattening it under her feet. She lunges again, takes a bit of a leap into another patch of ground cover, this made up of something bushy, scratchy, clawing the hell out of her legs. She walks delicately through it. She looks back, sees his flashlight sweeping the trees, the ground. Then off again.

Beside her, a thick tree grows with its roots exposed above the dirt. She jumps to that next, hugs herself to it. She skirts the bulk of it on tiptoe, walking along its bulging roots. With the tree between her and her pursuer, she presses herself off from it, another big lunge into more wild grass, and takes to fleeing again. It's not much, she thinks, but enough to require a bit more thorough investigation on his part. It's *time* she's buying herself, at the very least. So long as he doesn't manage to spot her directly, racing through the woods...

Not much farther ahead, she breaks from the trees and onto an open path. A dirt road. She looks both ways, uncertain which will take her to safety and which will take her back to the lake. It's difficult to tell in the dark, but she thinks there's a slight grade. *Down* must be the way back—down the mountain, back to civilization. How far must she run? She supposes it doesn't really matter. Best not to even think about it.

Just go. Just run.

She looks over her shoulder on occasion to see his light still flickering on and off through the distant trees. Thunder burbles through the clouds. A light rain mists over her face, her shoulders, as she hurries along. Her feet are sore, her ankles itching from all the prickly weeds and undergrowth.

She runs for what feels like five minutes or more, until finally she can't see his flashlight at all. She wonders if he's given up. Probably not. She imagines he would die before letting her get away, seeing as her escape would spell the end of him.

In the back of her mind, she hopes the other woman is all right. *Barbara.* Earnestly. If she's able to get away, Kylie hopes she can find help quickly enough to save her, too.

TWENTY-NINE

BARBARA

It hurts like hell to move, I'm so banged up. The basement is pitch black. I push myself onto my hands and knees in the dark, feel for the wall beside me, brace myself against it in order to get standing. Keeping to the wall, I shuffle ahead until my feet find the bottom stair. I touch around the wall some more, searching for a light switch. There isn't one. So instead I begin climbing the stairs. I climb to the door at the top, light shining in from underneath. I already know the door is locked but I try it anyway just to prove it to myself.

I slump down on the top step, lean against the door, and I listen.

I can hear Cassidy moving around the house. I hear her going through my things on the kitchen counter, the jingle of my own keys as she picks them up and takes them for herself.

"Cassidy," I say. I take a deep breath. I'm as reluctant to talk to her now as I am on a good day at work. Through the door, she stops whatever she's doing. Silence. Listening. So I continue. "Talk to me. Why are you doing this?"

Her footsteps draw near. Her shadow appears in the light under the door, standing just on the other side.

"Because you don't deserve it," she answers.

I have no idea what she means. She's doing this to me because… I don't deserve having this done to me? I'm confused, to say the least.

"What do you—"

"I work so much harder than you do," she goes on, cutting me off. "I meet all my deadlines. I never call in sick. I kiss everyone's ass all day long, every day of the week, and I see no gratitude for it. Not from anyone. It makes no sense why they'd choose you over me. Just because you've got seniority doesn't mean you work any harder than I do. You don't even have any *semblance* of interpersonal skills. I just don't get it…"

She pauses, long enough for my reeling mind to pick up the pieces of her words and understand what the hell she's talking about. It's so ludicrous, that even as I finally understand what she's going on about, I can hardly believe it.

"The promotion? That's… *that's* what this is about? Are you serious?"

It's a rhetorical question. Of course she's serious. The poisoned food, the gun she currently wields, throwing me down a set of stairs and locking me in her basement—it's crystal clear how serious she is. I watch the shadow under the door. Cassidy doesn't move, but she also doesn't respond.

"It's not my fault you didn't get the job, Cassidy. You

can't take this out on me…" Never mind that I'm trying to instill reason into someone with homicidal tendencies. "Besides, I thought you were happy for me? I thought…"

It dawns on me—Cassidy's little invitation to lunch that day. She'd already known I'd been offered the job. Or at the very least, she knew she *hadn't*. Listening to me vent about my life's problems, spilling my guts out about my daughter and my shaky marriage and everything else—she didn't care about any of that. Not really. This was the plan all along. To get me here, get rid of me, and take my place. It's vile, but it also strikes me as being rather… *shallow?* Hare-brained?

"What are you expecting to come of this, exactly?" I say. "You're going to get rid of me, and you think just like that, suddenly the higher ups will consider you for the job instead?"

The shadow under the door shifts around, as Cassidy shifts her weight from one leg to the other. She taps her foot, an audible *tap, tap, tap* on the hardwood floor outside.

"What happens after you're gone is none of your concern," she says. "Anyway, if you really think about it, Barbara, I'm doing you a favor here."

I say nothing, waiting for her to continue, but it seems she wants me to be an active listener. "A favor?"

"I've watched you these past couple of years. You know, since I've been with the company. I've seen the way you keep to yourself, how you mope around the office. You're like a zombie. Like you've never enjoyed a day in the sun in your whole life, in all your fifty years…"

Fifty years? I think. I'm not quite there yet. I almost want to correct her, but of course that's the least of my concerns right now.

"I can give you what you want," she goes on. "I can reunite you with your daughter."

Her words flatten me in an instant.

"You're insane," I tell her.

To my horror, Cassidy laughs on the other side of the door. I amuse her. She sounds almost *pleased.*

"Well, you might be right about that. It runs in the family…"

"What are you planning to do with me, then? Since poisoning didn't work out so well…"

"Once daddy takes care of that girl, we're going to take you for a nice, long drive somewhere in that car of yours. It'll be like you never came here. You left home, your husband, and vanished just like *that."*

Cassidy is so impressed with herself that she actually snaps her fingers on the other side of the door.

"I've been texting my husband all day," I tell her. "He knows I'm here. That I've *been* here."

This is a lie. Partially. Hank does not know where I am. Not the exact location, anyway. Call it stupidity, call it shortsightedness, but in the planning of this impulsive getaway—for which there was very little actual planning involved—I never told my husband the specific address for where I was headed. Not that it would do anyone a great deal of good, anyway, judging by how much my own GPS struggled to find this place. I did tell him the name of the lake itself—Little Reed Lake—but I won't hold it against him if he forgets.

"Yeah, well, people behave in all kinds of strange ways before they disappear," Cassidy says. "Or better yet, before they *off themselves.*"

My stomach churns at the thought. Hank would never believe such a thing, would he? Could he ever think me capable? Surely he knows I'm not in that bad a place. Not like that.

Am I losing you?

His words surface in my mind. My belly freezes cold.

"Either way, your stuff won't be here, and neither will you. Whatever you might have done here, wherever you might have gone after—it'll be an unsolvable mystery. Daddy's good at vanishing people."

Right on cue, before either of us can say anything more I hear the front door open. Cassidy's father arrives panting, out of breath, like he just ran the whole way back from wherever he went—wherever he chased the girl. I press myself against the basement door, listening even more intently.

"Daddy?" Cassidy says. "What happened? Did you get her?"

"No," Sterling answers. "I need your keys. Now."

"My keys?"

"Yeah, to your car. I need it."

"Did she get away?"

"She didn't *get away*," Sterling corrects, irritated at just the suggestion. "I know where she's headed. I'm pretty sure I know where she'll end up, too. If she's smart, she'll keep heading down the mountain. I just need to catch up to her before she reaches the main road…" Sterling trails off, distracted by something. "What is that? What happened? Where's the woman?"

"She's in the basement," Cassidy says, instilling her voice with a certain authority, like everything she's done so far has been perfectly sound, perfectly handled. "Everything's under control."

"Is that her phone?" Sterling asks. "Why is it all busted up on the floor like that?"

"It's nothing. I just thought… you know, better safe than sorry."

I'm overcome with the urge to interject—to do everything in my power to sow doubt in their minds. Panic. I can't resist.

"I spoke to my husband!" I shout through the door. "He knows I'm here, and he knows I'm in trouble!"

I really have no guarantee that Hank understood me over the phone. I shouted his name. I shouted that I needed help. I should have shouted 'call the police!' or something like that, but it's hard enough knowing what to say in regular conversation, let alone in moments of utter terror and desperation. I have no idea what he heard, or if he heard anything at all. For all I know, that call was a perfectly timed butt dial.

But in the interest of mental warfare, I announce this through the door like I'm absolutely certain.

"It's only a matter of time now!"

"What did she just say?" Sterling asks. I'm not sure if he's asking rhetorically. "She called her husband? How in the *hell*…"

"She didn't call anyone, daddy," Cassidy says. She

speaks hastily, obviously flustered. "I had her phone in my pocket, was all, and while I was escorting her to the basement it started to ring, and we had a little scuffle, you know. It was nothing serious, obviously. I handled it…"

"So she *didn't* speak to her husband?"

"I did!" I scream. "I spoke to him! I told him I was in trouble! He's sending help right now as we *speak!*"

"Cassidy?"

"She answered the phone for all of *two seconds,* daddy, I swear. I destroyed it before she could even *say anything.* She's lying."

Sterling goes quiet. Cassidy goes quiet, waiting for his response. I decide to be quiet as well, as I suddenly realize my side of the story might convince them to dispose of me now rather than later, if they believe they're running out of time.

"Fuck!" Sterling shouts suddenly, his voice booming. "God*dammit…*"

"The chance that her husband has the slightest idea—"

"Goddammit," Sterling repeats. "This is the last thing we need, Cass. The *last* thing."

"Chances are her husband has no idea what's going on! At the very least, this place is next to impossible to find. Even if her husband thought something might be wrong, we've got hours before anyone shows up…"

"I don't want *anyone* showing up," Sterling says. "Period."

Well, I think, if that were the case, then they made a huge mistake plotting my disappearance in this way. Obviously at some point my husband would wonder where I am, why I'm not answering his calls. He'd report me missing. He'd tell the police my general whereabouts, and mention my stay at *'a coworker's lake house.'* Cassidy would be questioned, no doubt. What's the plan then, I wonder? I'm tempted to ask. Maybe later, if I'm still alive and bored enough.

"We can't have police snooping around here, Cass," Sterling says, his thoughts circling the same place as mine.

"Well, we were *always* going to have police snooping a little," Cassidy says. "That part's inevitable…"

"Yes, but she's supposed to be long gone when they come looking. Along with all her stuff. It's supposed to look like she was never here, or at the very least like she left on her own. And what's this? What is *that*, Cass?"

"That's blood."

"Is that *her* blood? Why is there blood on the *goddamn floor*, Cass?"

"Daddy…"

"For Christ's sake… gimme the goddamn keys already." Cassidy's keys jangle as she hands them over. Sterling laughs, but I can tell there's not an ounce of humor behind it. "One thing at a time. One thing at a time…"

Sterling repeats this under his breath like a mantra, trying to keep his wits about him as his grown daughter seems committed to blowing everything up.

"You know, this wouldn't even be happening if you'd just kept your nose out of it," Cassidy says. "I had everything planned and under control before you decided to come—"

"We don't have time for this," Sterling says. His boots

clomp away toward the front door. "I'll be back with the girl. Do not, and I repeat, *do not* open that door under any circumstances."

"Of course. I'm not stupid…"

To this, Sterling simply laughs again, and suddenly the house gives a shake as the front door slams shut behind him. As soon as he's gone, Cassidy lets out a breath of relief. She returns to the basement door, her shadow slipping into the light. I sense her considering me, considering her options.

"You know, I'd put a bullet between your eyes right now," she says, "if it wouldn't make such a mess."

And with that, she turns away. I hear the noise of drawers being opened. The kitchen faucet runs for a moment. Then shortly after I hear what sounds like vigorous scrubbing—Cassidy washing my blood off the floor.

I gingerly touch my fingers to my head where she struck me with her gun, sticky with blood. Tender to the touch.

I suppose I'm lucky she chose that instead of the bullet between my eyes.

THIRTY

KYLIE

KYLIE SEES SOMETHING UP AHEAD, through the trees, away from the road. Another secluded property. A small, squat cabin. It's dark. Most likely vacant. She won't find any help there. She soon passes the turnoff that would otherwise take her to that property. She must be headed in the right direction, she thinks. She has to be getting close to a main road, at least. Somewhere. Eventually. If she can find *that*, something paved and *official*, she'll be one step closer to finding civilization, one step closer to finding a living, breathing soul who *isn't* a psychopath.

She fantasizes about this, seeing the headlights of an innocent passerby, flagging them down, begging them to help her, climbing into their car, driving off toward safety and putting this whole nightmare behind her...

She's so deep into this fantasy that when she hears car tires rolling gently behind her, she doesn't realize it's not just part of her imagination.

Then she really *hears* it—tires crunching over dirt and

tree debris, the soft whir of a car's engine. She nearly jumps out of her skin as she realizes. She turns to the sound, simultaneously stepping back toward the side of the road. She sees it, dark and prowling slowly along the road she's been following the last several minutes. Its headlights are off. A deliberate choice.

It's him.

Kylie steps off the road entirely. She hurries into the trees. He's already seen her, she thinks. He must have. Her best bet now is to flee deeper into the woods where his car can't follow. She surveys the surrounding woods, as well as the nearby property standing still and lonesome. She dashes for it. Something to hide behind, something to put between them and herself as she makes her escape.

As she continues toward the cabin, the stalking car turns from the dirt road, onto the private path, making its way toward the cabin likewise. That confirms it. He's seen her.

She abandons all pretense of stealth. She bolts into the trees, follows the downward slope of the woods, uses it to gain speed, knowing full well if she trips along the way it's going to hurt. From somewhere behind her, up the slope, there comes the slam of a car door. He's in pursuit again, on foot.

I'm not going back. I'm not going back, I'm not going back…

The storm's humid air clings to her like wet cobwebs, her feet gathering dirt and lacerations from the weeds and rocks as she hurtles onwards, downwards, as she leaps and dodges over various fallen branches and lumps of roots, arms out like wings for balance. The man says nothing, but she's certain she hears him, his gruff breath, his heavy footfalls gaining speed behind her. He's not a hulking man by any means, and yet Kylie feels him rolling toward her like some relentless avalanche she can't escape from, gathering speed, gathering *size* as he comes, massive in presence, in menace.

The hillside begins to flatten out. His movements grow louder. He's gaining on her, and fast. She practically feels him on top of her, feels his fingers reaching for her. A certain, terrible electricity builds between them, about to go off like lightning in the clouds. Kylie can hardly stand it anymore.

On the ground ahead, she spots a sizable branch, one she would otherwise jump over to continue in her flight. Instead she bends, swipes it into her hands, turning on her heel and brandishing the weighty, wooden pole across the darkness behind her.

"Stay away from me!" she screams.

The man nearly falls flat on his ass as he slides to a stop, avoiding the arc of her branch by mere inches. Kylie advances on him. She swipes the branch left and right. The man crab-scrambles backwards, narrowly avoiding her barrage. She brings the branch back over her shoulder and brings it down vertically. It thumps the dirt between his legs. He pushes himself standing. Kylie makes to swing again, but he's prepared this time. He catches the branch in both hands. He jerks it toward himself, tries to pry it from her grasp. As she staggers toward him, gripping the branch with all her strength, he plants the toe of his boot firmly in her gut and kicks her. *Hard.* She lets go of the branch then, launching backwards against another tree. Her head snaps back, knocks painfully. She collapses to her knees. For a moment, she's unsure if lightning flashes through the branches overhead or if she's seeing stars.

Before she can recover, the man moves over her, grabs her from behind, hooking his arms under hers. He proceeds to drag her away. Kylie wants to fight him, but her body is oddly loose, the connections between her brain and her limbs mushy. Dizzy. The back of her skull aches something fierce.

"Be a good little mouse," he whispers, panting tiredly back up the slope with her in tow. "I'm not ready to snuff you out just yet…"

It's only as they're cresting the hill that the fog in Kylie's mind begins to clear, and she becomes all too aware of just how exhausted she truly is. She fights a little harder. The man grabs hold of her a little tighter, wrapping his arms around her and hoisting her against himself. He carries her that way through the trees, wrestling with her like an unruly child. The vacant cabin stands dark and quiet beside them. Kylie grabs at his arms around her middle and presses, pulls, claws, to no avail. The car waits ahead of them. The man carries her to its rear, where he dumps her onto the ground, forces her down with one hand on the back of her neck while he pops open the trunk lid with the other.

"Get… off of me…"

He grabs hold of her again. She thrashes uselessly. He forces her into the trunk much too easily. She hates herself for this, for not being stronger, for not fighting harder, for being weaker than him. The fact she's been held captive for over a day with no food or water, or the fact she's exhausted herself swimming and running and fighting to her very last shreds of stamina, is no excuse in her mind.

The trunk slams shut on top of her. She pounds on it. Stupid. Pointless. Her muffled breath fills her ears and she hardly recognizes the sound of herself—hoarse, panicked, an animal in a cage. She searches the trunk's interior beneath the lid for an emergency lever of some kind but can find no such thing.

The car rumbles to life. She jostles in place as they begin rolling along the dirt road.

Back to the start.

THIRTY-ONE

BARBARA

I DON'T KNOW how much time I have left. I only know that I *will* run out of it eventually. The plan is to kill me, after all. I hope the girl gets away. I hope she leads Sterling on a wild goose chase, and buys me enough time to think of something. Or to *find* something around here, that I might use to assist in my own escape…

While Cassidy continues scrubbing up my blood from the living room, I turn to the darkness of the basement, the stairs below me. I search the wall beside the top of the stairway for a light switch but still can't find one.

Carefully, I navigate my way back down the steps. I pat the wall the whole way down. At the bottom, I search the wall there a second time, in case I missed the light switch the first. Failing that, I sweep the dark with both arms ahead of myself, hoping to find something, *anything*.

I find exactly what I'm hoping for.

My hand brushes a dangling chain. I grab it, pull it. It

plunges with a satisfying *clink*, and a bright bulb illuminates over my head. The basement is revealed.

And what a strange basement it is.

I stop for a moment, taking it all in. I expected to see some storage—shelves full of junk, boxes stacked in corners, some cobwebs and dust bunnies keeping each other company in the shadows.

Instead I find what appears to be *a fully furnished apartment.*

Immediately before me, near the bottom of the stairs, is a little kitchenette built along the opposite wall—a small refrigerator, a microwave, a tiny kitchen sink, and a modest amount of counter space. Beside the stairway, the basement opens into what can only be called a living area, with a small yellow loveseat—blotchy with stains and otherwise faded with time and dust—situated before a small entertainment center, a tiny television set on top. Across this space, the cramped basement is partitioned with a length of bookshelves, dividing the living area from whatever lays beyond.

For now, I'm rooted in place at the bottom of the basement stairs, unsure what the hell I've been thrown into down here. Literally *thrown* into.

In a mild daze, I peer back up the stairs, and what I see at the top, now revealed in the light, makes my blood run cold.

The basement door's surface is visibly *clawed.* A disturbing pattern of long scratches in the wood, with crimson smears that make my fingertips ache at just the sight of them.

Good lord…

So I look to the living area again instead. I force myself to move away from the stairs. I have to find something that can help me get out of here.

There's a lamp in the corner by the television set. I'm curious if it's plugged in and operational. I reach under the lamp shade, brushing its edge, which leaves a thick streak of dust along my wrist. I find the switch underneath. I give it a twist. The lightbulb comes on for a second before loudly *popping*—startling the hell out of me—and dying altogether.

Okay, not that.

I swim into the deepening dark, toward the wall of bookshelves. The shelves are fully stocked. I briefly glance along the titles and notice it's a lot of romance, along with some science fiction. At just a glance I notice several I've read myself, years ago. These are all rather old titles. This basement apartment, or whatever it is, doesn't seem to have been occupied in years. A couple decades, maybe, at least. I proceed around the bookshelves and into the second area behind them. It's entirely dark here, a pool of black. The ceiling groans as Cassidy moves around upstairs. I sweep my arms through the dark again, until I bump into the end of something with my legs. Hard, wooden. I change course, moving in the opposite direction, until I find another dangling chain. I blindly grab onto it. I give it a gentle tug, wincing as I do, anticipating another popping lightbulb. The light comes on, and *stays on*.

I scan my new surroundings and gasp.

"Oh my God."

Behind the bookshelf partition is what I can only

describe as a makeshift bedroom. A bed, at least. Not much else besides.

And someone is still lying in the bed.

My breath catches, my heart nearly slamming out of my chest.

I take a single step toward the bed—the foot of which I previously bumped into in the dark, a disturbance which had no effect on the occupant—and meet the cold, dark, empty gaze of the corpse lying under the covers. A woman's corpse. She's fully withered away, her leathery skin sucked against the skull underneath. Dark, scraggly hair falls around her face and shoulders. I imagine the pillow under her head is permanently misshapen after so many years. The bones of her hands are clasped over the covers, across her belly. An unfolded letter rests beneath them, as though she'd clutched the page to herself in her final moments. I know I should be searching for a weapon or some means of escape, but my curiosity gets the better of me. I stand over the poor dead woman, whom I assume left the scratch marks on the door at the top of the stairs, however long ago that must have been…

"My God," I mutter under my breath.

I take the page and gently pull it from her hands. It slides out easily, whispering against her bony fingers, as dry as the paper itself. With the letter in hand, I turn into the light and read what appears to be a child's scrawl.

It reads:

Dear mommy,

*I hope you feel better soon. Daddy says you are very sick
and contagis and he doesn't know when you will come
back home. I hope it's soon because my dance is next week
and I still need help practasing. Daddy doesn't know the
moves at all. Please get lots of sleep. I love you and I
miss you.*

Sincereley,
Cassidy

I'm not entirely sure why, but tears spring into my eyes.
I doubt it has much to do with this woman, or the woman
upstairs for that matter, but I'm holding back tears all the
same. Is it true, I wonder? Was this woman sick? With the
letter still in my hands, I look back and peer into the dark,
crusty depressions of her eyes. I doubt it was true, what
Cassidy's father told her. Perhaps it's the simple fact that
her mother's corpse is still down here. Not exactly how an
innocent *family man* would care for his sick wife, is it? I'm
curious how it's even possible that she's still here. Was
there not a funeral? Is she a missing person? Did she not
have any family looking for her? Parents? Siblings?

I wonder, does Cassidy even know the truth? I didn't
read much through the letters upstairs, the ones I found
stored in the bedroom closet. Had her mother written all
those letters down here? Surely Cassidy must know. She
has the key to the basement, after all.

Never mind all of this, I think. I should be looking for a
weapon.

I place the letter back on the bed with the body. I return

to the kitchenette, pull open several drawers, and discover children's utensils stored inside. Plastic spoons, forks, and plastic serrated knives that could hardly cut a meatloaf, I'm sure. I doubt I'm going to find much in the way of defense down here.

I also see no windows at all. However, I notice there are boards on the far wall, over the bed. They're plastered onto the concrete, possibly glued underneath as well. There's no way I can pry them off. This place has been made into a literal tomb.

I return to the stairs, to the basement door at the top. I sit on the top step. I can't help drawing my gaze over the deep scratches in the wood, and the blood, as I lean against the door and listen.

Cassidy must be finished scrubbing *my* blood from the floor. I can't hear her at all anymore. I listen very closely, holding my breath to do it.

"Cassidy?" I ask aloud.

"Have you finished your snooping, then?" she asks in reply, surprising me. She sounds as though she must be sitting at the kitchen counter just beyond the door. "I packed up all your stuff in the bedroom and noticed you'd done some snooping in there, too."

I hesitate, wondering what she means. Surely she couldn't have noticed…

"You went through my momma's letters. In the closet?"

I have no idea how she could tell. Unless she kept it stored very particularly, for precisely such a reason. Paranoia.

"Did you read them?" she asks.

"No," I answer truthfully. "I only skimmed one."

… I hope you're getting my letters…

… I miss you so much…

… I wish things were different…

… I wish I could see you…

… I can't say too much here, but…

In retrospect, what little I read of that letter could easily be interpreted as the careful wording of a prisoner, who isn't allowed to reveal they are in fact a prisoner. It occurs to me now I might be able to upset Cassidy, discussing these matters. Perhaps I can even stir up some resentment for her father, create a little more animosity between them amidst their unraveling plans?

"You know your mother wasn't actually sick," I say. "You know that, don't you?"

"Well," Cassidy says, "that depends on how you want to define *sick.* Was she *physically ill*? No, of course not…"

"Your father told you she was contagious…"

"And she was," Cassidy says. "In her way, she was."

"And how's that, exactly?"

"My daddy's also sick, you know," Cassidy says. I'm so tempted to say something sarcastic here, something antagonistic, but I refrain and let her continue. "He gets these… *urges."*

"He kidnaps and murders young women," I say. "And you help him do it."

"Yes, because that's what family does. That's what my momma couldn't understand. When she learned of my daddy's… *sickness*… she vilified him. Instead of trying to understand, she simply wished to ruin him…"

"What exactly is there to understand?" I say. "Your father is a murderer, Cassidy."

"He's a sick man," she says—except her tone is much less accusatory than how I might say it. Sympathetic, even. "He can't help what he is..."

"Other people are dying thanks to him. You don't think their lives matter? That girl out there, you don't think *her* life matters?"

"She's not my responsibility," Cassidy says. "Somebody else already failed her. It's unfortunate, but... it is what it is. You don't blame the wolf when somebody's sheep wanders from the pasture."

"Jesus, Cassidy..."

"My only concern is that my daddy is safe and provided for. Just as he provided for me when my momma turned her back on us."

Sitting at the top of the basement stairway, my vision is overcome by the image of the dead woman down below, mummified beneath her bedcovers.

"It could have been a lot worse for her," Cassidy continues. "My daddy did her a kindness, giving her this place, and letting her continue having a relationship with me."

I'm suddenly taken by another hot flash. Except, I'm not so sure that's all it is. It's accompanied by an intense, stormy, *seething* hatred inside of me, on behalf of the victim downstairs. What kind of mother-daughter relationship is that? Letters passed along by your abuser? Your murderer? A manipulative liar? How many letters did Cassidy's mother write which she never received, I wonder? And vice versa?

… I can't say too much here…

No doubt Sterling screened her mother's letters before delivering them, to ensure nothing too severe was ever implicated.

"You're an accomplice to murder, Cassidy."

"I'm a good daughter," Cassidy fires back without hesitation. "I'm sorry if you can't wrap your head around that… or that you'll never know what it's like to have one."

To this, my seething hatred amplifies. My blood boils.

"I had an incredible daughter," I say. "She was only seventeen when she was taken from me, and she was already ten times the woman you'll ever be."

Cassidy sighs, as though she's bored with this conversation. I hear the legs of her stool squeal against the floor as she stands up. Her feet lightly thump from the kitchen toward the other side of the house, where I imagine she peers out the window, waiting for her father to return with the girl.

God, I hope she gets away.

THIRTY-TWO

KYLIE

Kylie touches the back of her head where a nice, swollen goose egg has formed. Painful to the touch. She squirms around inside the trunk. She searches for an emergency lever again, but it's no use. They probably already saw to its removal, had there ever been one. You don't become a practiced kidnapper without investing in the proper precautions.

She searches the rest of the trunk instead. She happens upon a large canvas bag that's VELCRO'd to the floor of the trunk. An emergency car kit. She fumbles with it, finds the zipper, draws it open. She rummages around inside. She touches what feels like a coiled up jumper cable, some tow rope, a pair of grippy gloves, a hammer, a small plastic toolbox, a flashlight…

Just then the car hits a particular grade or divot and Kylie's weight shifts, pulling her toward the trunk door. The car bumps and rolls, shaking her like a bug in a can.

Then it levels out. She pulls herself beside the emergency bag again.

She grabs the flashlight. She presses the tiny rubber button and it shines to life—a bright, sterile white beam. She uses it to search the rest of the bag. She takes out the hammer as well and sets it aside as a possible weapon. There's an additional vinyl bag within the kit, which she opens and discovers a miniature pair of scissors, a tire gauge, a screwdriver. She takes the screwdriver. Then she opens the plastic toolbox, where she finds an array of Allen wrenches, along with some other odds and ends. Nothing that will beat the hammer and screwdriver, though.

The man, her captor, has become sloppy. Throwing her in here like this, untied, with free reign to the trunk's contents? He must be desperate, she thinks. In a hurry. She hopes he's still in a hurry when he opens the trunk again and she lands a blow to his head with a hammer.

With her weapons in hand, Kylie inches back toward the trunk door. She curls up there, blinks her blind eyes in the dark, taking deep breaths. The car continues to gently rock her in place.

Perhaps it's a lack of sleep, along with everything else, but her mind wanders easily.

She's reminded of another time she was stuck in a cramped, dark place like this. It was their father's birthday. Kylie and her sister had stationed themselves in his bedroom closet, waiting for him to come home from work so they could surprise him. It was her sister's idea mostly. Kylie was only a small girl then. Six? Seven? Her sister had even wrapped a present for their father—a pack of baseball cards, which their father collected at the time—and left it on his bed. The idea was that he'd see the present first, open it, and then they'd jump out and surprise him with a big, jolly *'Happy birthday!'*

What happened instead, was they stood in his closet for an entire hour before finally Kylie's sister stepped out and checked the garage to confirm he still hadn't come home. Then they spent the next *two hours* moseying about the house, alone, waiting for his headlights to spill across the windows in the front room so they could hurry and take up their hiding spot again.

Kylie vividly remembers asking her sister: *'what if he doesn't come home?'* Because that had happened once before, on the weekend, when they'd been left alone for an entire forty-eight hours.

On this particular night, however, eventually he *did* come home. His headlights *did* spill across the windows, and Kylie and her sister ran to his bedroom closet again, even though the wait had already mostly drained them of their excitement.

After all, he was coming home late, and that usually only meant one thing.

Sitting in the pitch-black trunk, Kylie replays it all in her mind—holding her breath alongside her sister as they watched through the slats in the closet door, as their father stumbled into his bedroom, not even noticing the gift they'd left him on his bed as he collapsed on top of it and passed out.

Kylie almost threw the closet door open to yell out *'Surprise!'* but was luckily stopped by her sister with a firm hand on her wrist. In the dark closet, her sister shook her head adamantly: *No.* If they tried to surprise their father then, they wouldn't like which version of him they got. So instead they slipped out quietly, closed the bedroom door behind themselves, and got themselves ready for bed on their own.

If their father ever discovered their gift the next morning, he never mentioned it. And neither Kylie nor her sister ever asked.

Kylie's wandering mind snaps back into her skull as the car slows. It comes to a complete stop. The engine audibly falls silent. She holds very still and listens as the door opens and shuts, as heavy boots walk the length of the car. She grips the hammer tight in one hand, the screwdriver in the other. The hammer feels more lethal in her grasp, more weighty, so she favors it in her dominant hand. She readies herself as the footsteps get louder beside the trunk, prepared to spring out like a jack-in-the-box.

Surprise!

Then those footsteps fade with distance. Gone.

She lets out the breath she was holding.

That's okay, she thinks.

Just like waiting for her father to come home drunk after a late evening at the bar… Kylie's got all night.

THIRTY-THREE

BARBARA

THROUGH THE DOOR, I hear what sounds like an utterance of relief from Cassidy. The front door opens. Then silence for a time.

"You get her?" Cassidy says. I can only barely hear her. She must be standing on the porch outside, which means Sterling must be back already. Heavy footsteps move into the house which are clearly his. My heart sinks.

"Where's your tape?" Sterling says.

"Tape?"

"Duct tape."

"Oh. It's in the drawer by the kitchen sink. I'm guessing you got her then?"

Sterling doesn't answer Cassidy's question. Instead he makes his way across the house, coming closer to the basement door on his way to the aforementioned kitchen drawer. I listen closely as he pulls it open, rummages for a moment, then begins making his way back.

"You got her?" Cassidy asks again.

"Yeah, I got her. I'm gonna need your help getting her tied up, though."

"Oh..." Cassidy sounds disappointed. "You didn't already do it?"

"No, I didn't." Sterling's footsteps come to a complete stop suddenly. "On second thought..."

He retraces his footsteps back into the kitchen, back toward *me*, at the basement door. His shadow slips into the light underneath.

"Do you have any idea what she's even up to down there?"

"I'm right here," I answer. His shadow visibly flinches, which gives me just the slightest thrill, the slightest satisfaction. "I don't know what you do for a living, Sterling, but you and your daughter should both keep your day jobs. Not that Cassidy's any better at hers."

"Funny," Sterling answers. Deadpan. Then, to Cassidy he says, "Let's deal with her first."

I don't know why I egg him on like that. Now has got to be the worst time to be cheeky, but somehow I can't help myself. I'm angry this is even happening. I'm scared, too, of course. Terrified. My head still aches from being pistol whipped, my body still aches from being tossed down the stairs. I've been told rather plainly that I'll be dead before the night is through. So why do I egg them on? Maybe it's a bizarre coping mechanism. Maybe I'm just not any good at this whole *self-preservation* thing...

"What's the plan?" Cassidy asks.

"The plan is that you help me with her. Can you handle that?"

Even I can hear the sound Cassidy makes in response to her father's sharp implication—a disbelieving scoff with a wounded edge.

"Yes, I can *handle* that."

"All right, then. We need to hurry."

"Daddy... nobody's showing up any time soon. You don't need to be so—"

"I don't care if anyone *is* or *isn't* showing up anytime soon, Cass. We need to be *smart* right now. Smarter than we've been. Now are you ready to help, or do I have to do this myself?"

"All right," Cassidy says. "I just want to understand what the plan is, that's all..."

"First, we're going to tie this bitch up. Then we're going to tie that *other bitch out there* up. Then we're going to take them both someplace where nobody's going to find them."

"Where's that?"

To this, Sterling practically *growls* with irritation. "Let's just get this over with, shall we? Hold this for a second..." He steps right up against the basement door. I can sense him considering me through it. "Barbara?"

Should I run back down the stairs, I wonder? Grab a plastic fork from the kitchen drawer to defend myself?

I stand up where I am, on the top step, anticipating them. Sterling's shadow is joined by Cassidy's as she hovers behind him while he unlocks the door. The keys jingle faintly as Sterling works one into the lock. The lock clicks. I take a single step back, onto the next stair below—a defensive stance. Stable. My every muscle tightens, coiling into springs. Their shadows shift around a bit, as Sterling gets ready to open the door.

What are my options here?

The door pulls open abruptly. I flinch back—but so does Sterling on the other side. It happens so quickly. Something inside me, some instinctive, inner-animal part of me catches the look on Sterling's face: the uncertainty, the *fear*. Whatever my options might be, my body chooses all on its own. I reach for the man in front of me, grab him by the shirt, get two good handfuls of it, twisting it up into my fists as I pull him toward me with all my strength, all my weight, pivoting on both my feet which I've got placed sturdily on different steps. Despite Sterling's own caution, I manage to catch him by surprise. After all, I'm just some *stupid bitch* he has to *deal with.* He expected nothing and I'm giving him a whole lot more than that.

Sterling gropes at me as I pull him through the open door, but it's merely a reflex. His fingers graze my arm. I don't even have to pull him very far. He staggers across the basement door's threshold, his foot finds the next step down, but there's hardly room for it there beside my own. His boot scuffs the step's edge, sliding down to the next, and in an instant he's falling, *rolling* down the steps just like I did earlier. Cassidy utters some gasp or shout of surprise. I'm lucky she's not holding her gun, or she might have pulled the trigger already. As her father hits the floor at the bottom of the stairway, I lunge for her next. She tries to close the door on me, before I barge it against her. I throw her sprawling onto the kitchen floor, the duct tape in her hand rolling away.

Now what? Now where? My mind is spinning, frozen with indecision. From the corner of my eye I see Cassidy's keys still dangling from the doorknob. I grab them, rip them loose. As Cassidy scrambles back onto her feet, I vaguely search the room for her gun, knowing she must have set it down somewhere. But I don't see it. Then Cassidy is upright. That's when I finally do see it—as she pulls the gun from the back of her waistband. I bolt for the front door, which is standing wide open.

Dear God, what the hell am I doing?

I'm panicking. I'm trying to survive.

It's so incredibly easy to watch a movie and roll your eyes at the decisions being made on screen by characters in peril. It's another thing entirely to be in such peril yourself. Instincts take over. It's autopilot. You don't have time to make sound decisions. You just make them or you don't.

I don't know what kinds of decisions I'm making as I escape onto the front porch, rattle down the steps, and make a mad dash for Cassidy's parked car. Cassidy screams from inside. I can't tell if she's screaming at me, or screaming for her father. Then I hear footsteps on the porch behind me. Big, booming feet. They're not Cassidy's foot-steps, they're Sterling's. I yank the car door open, climb inside, pull it shut, and fumble my hand across the buttons on the inside of the door in search of the lock. But before I can find it, the door yanks back open beside me. Sterling grabs me by the bicep. His grip is *hard*. Crushing. I can hardly resist him as he drags me out and onto the dirt, where he wastes no time driving the toe of his boot into my stomach. All the air *whooshes* out of me in an instant.

"You stupid fucking bitch," he says. He kicks me again. I wheeze.

I know I don't *deserve* this, not any of it, but I also understand why the sick bastard whom I just threw down a set of stairs is upset with me.

As I choke for air, curling in on myself in the dirt from the ache in my guts, Sterling grabs the keys from my weak grasp. Cassidy arrives rather awkwardly behind him, sliding to a halt with her gun in both hands, huffing and puffing and scowling viciously, like she'd *wanted* to help, if only she'd been able to show up in time…

"We should just kill her now, daddy," she says. "Be a whole lot easier for us."

"A whole lot easier?" Sterling says. He's panting from the chase. "Easier how, exactly?"

"Well," she says, and pauses. "Because then at least we wouldn't have to fight her every step of the way, and—"

"And leave her DNA all over the place," Sterling interjects. "Yeah, let's give the investigators all the forensic evidence they could ever hope for! Great idea!"

Cassidy falls silent. Meanwhile I'm still writhing in pain, too incapacitated to continue fighting.

"Where's the duct tape?" Sterling asks.

Without a word, Cassidy hurries back inside to retrieve it. When she returns, she hands it to Sterling, then stands back to watch as he pushes me over with his foot, squashing me down onto my stomach with his boot atop the small of my back. He crouches, rips a length of tape.

"Grab her hands for me," he tells his daughter.

Cassidy does as he says. At this point I don't even resist.

I don't have the energy. Cassidy pins my arms painfully behind me as Sterling wraps the duct tape around my wrists several times over, nice and tight. Then he moves to my feet. I feel his hands on my ankles—large, strong, rough. He wraps my ankles in duct tape likewise.

"Okay, so…" Cassidy's tone suggests nervousness, hesitation, walking on eggshells. "What's the plan again?"

Sterling stands up with a heavy sigh.

"I'm going to take them someplace nobody will find them."

"And where's that?"

"I'm not telling you where," he says. "Should the worst happen, the less you know, the better."

"Are you going to kill them?" There's something in Cassidy's voice that sounds like disappointment, like she was hoping to be more involved, or at the very least, a witness to her father's crime. She craves it—my downfall. Never in a million years would I have guessed she hated me so much.

"That's enough talk for now," Sterling says. "Let's get the girl tied up next."

I turn my face against the dirt to see them as they come to stand at the trunk of Cassidy's car.

"She's wily as hell," Sterling says. "So be ready." He turns to his daughter, looks her up and down as she steps in with the gun aimed on the trunk. "Don't fucking shoot her, Cass. Put that thing away. Hell, why do you even *have* that…"

"What do you mean? You own a gun."

"For emergencies only," Sterling replies. "They're far too messy otherwise."

"Well, is this not an emergency? It feels like one to me…"

"Would you just put it away? You're making me nervous."

Cassidy reluctantly tucks the gun into the back of her waistband again. Sterling presses the button on her key fob. The trunk pops open, only an inch or so. For a moment, nothing happens. Sterling doesn't make any immediate move. Cassidy stands at the ready. Then, pulling back a little, Sterling reaches and pushes the trunk upward, as if he expects something to—

For a moment, I think an animal has been set loose. The girl springs up from the trunk with a deep gravel in her voice I never would have thought possible. A vicious snarl. She swipes the darkness between them. The hammer she wields winks prettily. As it fails to reach Sterling, she lunges with her opposite hand, coming down vertically with yet another weapon in its grasp. Sterling catches her by the wrist, only barely, the screwdriver's tip inches from his shoulder. She swings the hammer a second time. It connects, striking him in the ribs. Sterling's lips pull back, baring his teeth. He drops the roll of duct tape as he steps into the girl, butts his head against hers. The girl's head snaps back and all at once her nose is a bloody mess. Sterling forces her backward, pushes her against the open trunk door. Cassidy bounces anxiously from side to side, no help at all.

"Get her daddy!" she screams.

The girl tries to swing the hammer a third time, but this time Sterling grabs it, yanks it from her fist. He throws it carelessly to the ground, then hauls her out of the trunk and onto the ground likewise. The girl struggles to get her feet beneath her, scraping and sliding in dirt. She scrambles onto her knees, her screwdriver-wielding hand still secured in Sterling's grip. He wrenches her wrist so that she screams. The screwdriver falls to the ground. He forces her down, manhandles her onto her stomach.

"Cass?" he says through gritted teeth.

"Right here, daddy..."

Cassidy swipes the fallen duct tape off the ground. She pulls a new length, gets down beside her father and the girl, and helps to wrap up her wrists. The girl flails and bucks.

"You settle down now," Sterling says in a rough whisper. "You'll just make this harder on yourself..."

"I don't care," the girl whimpers. She snorts back tears. "I don't care..."

It's then she catches sight of me, turns still. She stares at me with a certain kind of pain, a certain kind of shame, like she's embarrassed not to have gotten away. For an instant, I do wonder how she managed to get herself caught again, out there in the woods with all that darkness to hide her. But it's not her fault. None of this is her fault. Nobody should have to fight something like this. *Survive* something like this... *God*, I hate the fear I see in her eyes. The abject terror.

Sterling holds her down while Cassidy moves onto her ankles, doing her up just like me.

"So you're really not telling me where you're taking them?" Cassidy says, standing up.

"You've no reason to know." Sterling stands as well, though he grimaces as he does. Even from a few feet away I can hear his knees pop with the effort. I know the feeling. "Besides, I need you here to start doing clean up. *Major* fucking clean up."

"I already cleaned up her blood, daddy. There's not—"

"Collect all her stuff. Every single thing she brought with her. Put it back into her car. Get the house tidy, like she was never here. When I get back, we'll go for a nice long drive."

"How long do you think you'll be? Until you're back, I mean?" Cassidy asks.

"I don't know. Not long."

"My husband knows I'm here," I remind them, in case they've forgotten. "He's already sent help, I'm sure of it. Whatever you plan to do with me, with us, you won't get away with it. It's already over for you. I promise."

Sterling comes to stand next to me, his boots crunching the dirt just next to my head.

"Whatever help *may* or *may not* be coming, there won't be anything to find once it gets here. It's going to look like you packed up and disappeared all on your own. You, your car, your things, will vanish. Believe me, I know what I'm doing. I've done it plenty before."

"Are you going to kill her?" Cassidy asks.

"Will you stop asking me that already? What do you think?"

Cassidy folds her arms, pops her hip. "I don't know

what you're being so ornery for, daddy. None of this is my fault."

Sterling sighs quietly under his breath. "Nothing's ever your fault, sweetheart..."

"Huh? And what's that supposed to mean?"

"Nothing. It doesn't mean anything. Help me get these two into the trunk."

"Oh. You're taking my car, then?"

Sterling throws his hands in the air, looking around them in a mocking fashion.

"Well, I'm not putting them in the open bed of my truck, am I? And seeing as how I'd *really love it* if you'd get started on packing up her shit while I'm gone, that only leaves your car, right?"

"Okay, okay. Jesus..."

I watch as they stoop over the girl, Sterling with her upper body, Cassidy lifting her by the legs. Despite the hopelessness of it, the girl continues thrashing in their arms, making their task as frustrating as possible. I admire her for that. I really do. Myself, on the other hand, I fully grasp the futility of fighting at this stage. I'm not going to wriggle my way out of the duct tape around my wrists and ankles, nor am I going to thrash my way out of Cassidy's and Sterling's plans for me.

After they finish dumping the girl back inside Cassidy's trunk, they come for me next. Sterling lifts me by the crooks of my armpits. Cassidy lifts me by my ankles. I meet Cassidy's gaze as she bends and scoops me up, and she has the nerve to *smile*, a devilish little smirk at the corner of her mouth. She's enjoying this.

"Cassidy," I say, as I'm lifted up off the dirt. "Getting rid of me isn't going to land you a promotion. You're not helping yourself here. This is a mistake, I'm telling you…"

"Aw, you must be feeling pretty desperate," she says. She pants as she and her father carry me to the trunk of her car. "Don't worry, Barb. A month from now, nobody at the office will even remember you're gone."

They dump me into the trunk carelessly, right on top of the girl, who whimpers as I land on top of her. I shrug away as she does the same. I roll onto my back, peering up from the trunk and into the branches, into the storm. Lightning flashes somewhere up there, blooming in the black clouds. Before I get to hear the thunder, however, Sterling slams the trunk shut and seals us into the muffled darkness.

THIRTY-FOUR

BARBARA

WE SIT IN THE DARK. I can't see anything, but I can smell something. A few things, really. I smell what must be my own body odor. What might also be the girl's body odor. Then there's something else underneath, something pleasant I can't place, but know can't be mine. It's fragrant. Shampoo? I only catch a whiff of it for a moment before the scent of our sweat and fear overwhelms me again, but I'm sure it must have been her scent, perhaps some hair product peeking through despite the hours—days?—she's been held in captivity.

The scent immediately reminds me of *her*. An olfactory reflex. In the dark, my mind fills with images of my daughter's bathroom counter, overflowing with skincare products, the mirror steamed up from the shower, the muggy air billowing with sweet scents as she rushes to get ready for another night out with her friends. Perhaps the very last night out with her friends…

I can also hear the girl, now and again. She cries softly beside me. I think she's trying to cry softly, privately. If I wasn't sharing this cramped cage with her, she'd be sobbing more openly, I'm sure. I'm tempted to say something—something reassuring like *'everything's going to be okay'* or *'it's all right, you're all right'* but I refrain. Not only am I a complete stranger to her, but she's old enough to know better.

We are not all right. Everything is not going to be okay.

There's movement. The sound of a car door slamming shut. The vibration of the engine starting. The car starts to move. We rock and slide on either half of the trunk as we travel out of the clearing, up the winding path from Cassidy's lake house into the woods. The start of our journey is enough to stifle the girl's sobs.

I still can't believe this is happening. I thought people like Cassidy only existed in the movies. Or at the very least, only in the documentaries, in *other people's lives,* not mine. Then there's Sterling. The girl beside me knows more about him than I do, certainly. She's probably had all these same thoughts.

I can't believe this is happening.

I try to imagine where he's taking us. Someplace far from the lake, where we won't be found. But he also told Cassidy he wouldn't be gone long. So which is it? Someplace far away, or someplace close enough that he won't be gone long? I also can't wrap my head around why he refused to tell Cassidy whether or not he planned to kill us. Given the fact that Cassidy seemed eager to put a bullet in our heads, her father's reluctance to confirm his intentions tells me maybe he's *not* so eager to finish us off. Not yet, anyway. And why might that be? I don't know. Maybe I'm entirely off course.

We continue to bump around on what must be endless dirt roads for a while. We're also faced with several inclines which push both the girl and I toward the trunk door, the girl helpless not to squish against me there.

"Sorry..." she breathes, as she fights tooth and nail to slide away from me.

I'm touched that she's apologizing at all in this situation.

We must be heading farther into the hills. Judging by the way my weight shifts from one direction to the other, leveling out temporarily only to be faced with another incline, we're driving up some kind of switchback. Then the slope evens out a bit, becomes gentler, more gradual. Still a dirt road, however.

For a short distance, the road becomes much less bumpy. Then we come to a stop.

I estimate the drive was about thirty minutes, there-abouts. Hard to tell exactly. Now we're stopped, I can hear the light patter of rain on the trunk door. The girl and I both hold our breath to listen as Sterling's footsteps come around the rear of the car. The trunk door opens, lifts up, reveals him standing in the red glow of taillights. A handsome monster. Behind him, the storm flashes with lightning, followed by a dangerously quick crack of thunder.

Sterling reaches over me, grabs the girl, and proceeds to drag her out of the trunk first. The girl lets loose a string of expletives against him, shimmying in his arms. Sterling says nothing in return. He simply pulls her out onto the ground and drags her elsewhere. I can't see much from inside the trunk. I see more lightning through the surrounding branches. Light rain sprinkles my face. I hear what sounds like the shrill creak of old hinges nearby. Shortly after, Sterling reappears before me. He leans into the trunk, puts his hands on me. I fight a little. Not much, but a little. Not enough to matter, really. Sterling hauls me out of the trunk and onto the weedy, muddy ground. With his hands under my armpits, he drags me backward, his feet shuffling. All I see are the trees and the darkness in our wake. I crane my neck to try and peer at where we're headed, where Sterling's dragging me. I glimpse it only for an instant—a wooden structure caught in the headlights, standing square and dripping wet under the trees.

A shed.

Distant thunder rumbles across the sky as Sterling brings me through the open door, from one darkness into another. He dumps me next to her again, side by side on our backs. I sit upright as Sterling moves to leave. He turns to face us in the doorway, a black shape in the headlights, the flickering storm.

"Your husband will never find you here." Though I can't see Sterling's face, I can *hear* the smile in his voice. He takes a deep breath, sighs pleasantly. He passes his hand along the door frame beside him, rubbing the wood affectionately. "This place sure takes me back. Anyway. You two sit tight. I'll be back before you know it."

He shuts the door on us. I hear something rattle on the other side—the thump of a padlock against the door. Then his footsteps retreat. The car door slams shut. I listen as the tires pull around through the soft mud and underbrush and he begins his journey back, out of earshot.

All we're left with is the rain on the roof, the thunder in the skies.

THIRTY-FIVE

KYLIE

AFTER EVERYTHING she's been through, Kylie's exhausted. She's amazed she was able to go as far as she did, to keep fighting as hard as she did. Yet it still wasn't enough.

"I should have kept running," she says. She says it loud enough the woman beside her twitches in reply, surprised.

"What do you mean?"

What does Kylie mean? She supposes her statement could mean a few different things.

She should have kept running that night. She shouldn't have stopped and sat on that sidewalk, waiting for any stranger to come along and feign concern.

She should have kept running once she reached the other side of the lake. She shouldn't have gone inside with Barbara when that psycho's daughter showed up. They cornered themselves. Of course, neither of them could have possibly known what was coming. Barbara knew even less than she did.

"I don't know what I mean," Kylie answers. "Maybe... maybe I shouldn't have run in the first place..."

"You had to run," Barbara says. "You did the right thing."

She has no idea what Kylie's really talking about. How could she? Kylie takes a great deep breath as she loses herself in the shadows overhead, swirling under the roof, under the pattering rain. She imagines everything again in that darkness, replays it with gut-wrenching clarity.

"I ran away from home two nights ago," she tells her. "That's when they found me. I thought... I thought..."

She already told Barbara this—about Cassidy, about the man in the backseat. She drifts off, realizing she's only repeating herself, even as her mind's eye continues to cruelly dangle those regrets before her—the smiling woman behind the wheel, the sudden movement from the backseat, the bulging muscles of his arms as he choked her out from behind. She remembers coming to briefly, as the man fed her something from a spoon, something like cough syrup. Maybe it even *was* cough syrup. She'd already swallowed most of it by the time she was cognizant again. Then came the bag over her head. And then...

"It's not over yet," Barbara says. "You're not alone here. There's two of us."

Kylie fidgets in place, and winces at the pain in her shoulders, her neck, having been tied up like this for so long already, with her arms behind her back.

"Two of us," she repeats. "And what does that matter? What are we supposed to do?"

"Well…" Barbara has to think for a minute. "First we should try getting out of our binds."

Kylie strains her wrists against the duct tape, entertaining the notion despite her despair. It's tight, obviously. But it's not the twine she was previously tied with. And although she's pretty sure she's not strong enough to rip herself out of it anytime soon, there are two of them, like Barbara said. This gives Kylie an idea.

"Are you on your back?" Kylie asks.

"Yes," Barbara says. "Why?"

"Roll over. So I can get at your hands."

Barbara doesn't waste any time. She does exactly as Kylie says.

"Okay. I'm on my stomach."

Kylie gets onto her knees. She waddles toward Barbara until she bumps against her. With her own hands behind her back, there's little else she can use to navigate the dark. She knows this will be weird for the both of them, but what other choice is there? She bends over, touches her face to Barbara's arms. Once she feels them—the smooth knob of Barbara's elbow against her cheekbone—she quickly slides her face down until she finds the duct tape around Barbara's wrists. She pauses there.

"I'm gonna chew through your duct tape," she warns.

"What?" Barbara sounds *vaguely* stunned, like Kylie's just suggested something absurd. "You'll break a tooth doing that."

"I don't think so," Kylie says. "And besides, who cares? How else are we supposed get out of our binds, like you said?"

It *was* Barbara's suggestion. What else did she expect?

Sorry if I bite you by accident, Kylie thinks but doesn't say.

She finds the edge of the tape along Barbara's forearm —however many layers it's been wrapped, she has no idea —and gets to biting. It's more difficult than she expected. For starters, her mouth is much less nimble than her fingers. Then again, her fingers aren't nearly as sharp as her teeth...

"Hold on a second," Barbara says.

Kylie lifts up momentarily, listens as Barbara fidgets in the dark, moving her arms this way and that.

"Okay," she says. "I just thought... maybe if I could wrinkle the tape, stretch it out a bit..."

Kylie's not sure if Barbara's efforts helped any, but she resumes gnawing and biting at the tape, pulling with her teeth until the edges are breaking, tearing little by little. It's actually working, even if her teeth aren't quite as strong as she assumed. Barbara might be right. Maybe she *could* break her teeth doing this, but Kylie doesn't care. What are a few broken teeth if it means not being carved up by a psychopath? It's impossible to tell for sure, but she thinks she's got it halfway done already.

"Oh my God," Barbara says. "I think you're getting it. Hold on a second..."

Kylie lifts up again. On the ground, Barbara fidgets around some more, writhing in place. Suddenly Kylie hears the tearing, the popping of the reinforced threads in the tape.

"I think..." Barbara sits up entirely. Kylie scoots away from her, making room. "I think..."

Barbara strains a bit more, until there comes the final *snap* of the tape tearing in two.

"I did it," Barbara says. "*We* did it. Here, turn to me now. Give me your hands..."

Kylie swivels, turning her back to Barbara as Barbara's hands fumble over her. She finds the tape around Kylie's wrists and begins to pry at it.

"Shit," she says. "It's harder than I thought."

"Maybe you can rip it just a little with your teeth," Kylie offers.

Barbara thinks about it. "All right. Hunch over a little..."

Kylie hunches all the way over, her hands lifting against the small of her back. Barbara takes hold of her hands, lifts them a little toward her mouth. The position is a little painful, with Kylie's shoulders already pulled back like they are. Barbara uses her hands to pull the tape away from Kylie's wrist as much as possible before chewing into it. Kylie hears the *snap, snap, snap* of Barbara's teeth plucking at the tape.

"There," Barbara says.

She begins pulling again. This time the tape begins ripping with ease. In no time at all, it tears in half and Kylie's hands are free. She straightens, feels the immediate relief in her shoulders.

"All right, now let's get our feet..."

The shed falls into a prolonged, muffled silence as they each work on their own ankles, pulling and picking at their tape. Through the gentle drone of rain, thunder booms. Every now and then, Kylie glimpses light shining through gaps in the shed's wooden planks, as lightning illuminates the woods outside.

Barbara gets her tape off before Kylie does.

"There, I got mine. You need help?"

"No," Kylie says. "I think I've almost got it…"

The main trouble was getting the first tear started. It might have been quicker to just use their teeth again. Nevertheless, Kylie manages to rip a portion of the tape. From there, pulling the rest in half is fairly easy, though she winces as she peels the tape away from her sore ankles, made raw from the previous twine.

"I got it," she announces.

Barbara is already standing, feeling her way around the shed's perimeter. Kylie reaches into her pocket and produces what she's sure will be a welcome surprise—the flashlight from Cassidy's trunk. She presses the rubber button, casting its white beam against the rough, splintery wood.

"Where'd you get that?" Barbara asks.

"In that lady's trunk. Same bag I found the hammer and screwdriver…"

Kylie shines the light all around them, from one empty corner to the next. It's just an empty shed, with nothing but them stored inside. She shines the light on the shed door, which Barbara pushes against.

"It's locked with a padlock on the other side, I'm pretty sure."

"What do you think this place is?" Kylie asks. She stands up likewise, shines the light up at the roof, where she sees moisture has leaked through in the back corner, darkening the wood there.

"I think it's just a shed," Barbara says.

"I know that, but…" Kylie shines the light across the floor, then holds the trembling beam on what she finds. "Shit. Yeah. That's kinda what I thought."

Barbara lets out a little gasp when she sees it. The blood-stains on the floor. *Old*, old blood, but blood all the same.

"It's a murder shed," Kylie states plainly, which sounds silly to say, even if it's an accurate description.

"Before, you said they picked you up off the side of the road," Barbara says. "Were you hitchhiking?"

"No, not exactly," Kylie says. "I was just… sitting there, minding my own business. But I did need a ride, so I guess kinda, yeah. I'm not the first one he's taken, either. Not by a long shot. There was another woman down there with me, in the basement. A body, I mean. She was already dead."

"Jesus…"

"He dumps them in the lake."

Kylie can still picture those other bodies she glimpsed, wrapped in tarps under the lake dock. How many had there been? She didn't really get a long look at them. A blink-and-you'll-miss-it lightning strike. But there had been several.

"He doesn't want to kill us off right away," Kylie goes on, "because he wants to save us for later."

Barbara pushes against the shed door again, rattling the padlock on the other side.

"This shed is old," she says. "Maybe if we can… I don't know…"

Kylie thinks she understands. She approaches the shed door alongside Barbara.

"Move."

Even in the fringes of the flashlight's glow, Barbara looks visibly dubious. But she stands aside all the same. With just her bare foot, Kylie kicks the shed door. Once. Twice. Each time the door bangs loudly, stopped short by the lock, which seems to be holding strong despite the obvious age of this place.

"Well, nothing can ever be so easy," Barbara says.

They both tense to a deafening crack of thunder. The rain seems to instantly thicken, pelting the roof like pebbles, loud and heavy.

The storm outside is only growing stronger.

THIRTY-SIX

BARBARA

As we pace around the shed's perimeter like two pent-up cats, the girl gives the shed door another few kicks here and there, on the off chance a previous kick weakened something. For all we know, the metal plate through which the padlock is looped is only another five or six kicks away from pulling loose. Or perhaps the lock itself is old, rusted, ready to fall apart at the next slightest vibration.

Every now and then I get a good look at her, as she aims the flashlight so that her face becomes visible in the peripheral glow, and each time I'm struck by her youth. She's young. Too young to endure anything like this. I want to tell her how sorry I am she's going through this, how sorry I am that she's had to see the things she's seen.

The world isn't all like this, I promise.

I want to drill into her the fact that life gets better, but of course, these circumstances are not part of the average life. And even so, despite what's happening to us *right now*, who am I to claim that life gets better, anyway? Sometimes it gets worse.

Eventually we tire of pressing ourselves to the shed walls and take a break, sitting down on the dusty floor across from each other. The girl aims her flashlight at the ground between us, where the largest pool of blood once gathered, staining those boards darker than all the rest. She seems to fixate on those stains, staring through them into faraway places.

"What's your name?" I ask her, hoping to distract us both. Also, it's only just occurred to me that I haven't learned her name yet.

"Kylie," she says. Her voice is flat. Listless.

"Oh, well, it's nice to meet you, Kylie," I say. I mean it to sound tongue in cheek, but obviously she's not in the mood for humor. Why would she be? "I'm Barbara."

"I know," she says. She doesn't take her eyes off the blood. "I heard that crazy bitch call you that earlier."

"Right. Cassidy…" I chew the inside of my lip, watching her watching the blood. I know it's not really my responsibility to worry on her behalf, but I do. I hate the look in her eyes. It's different than the fear I saw earlier, on the dirt outside Cassidy's lake house. Now her gaze is as deadened as her voice, the dried blood between a reminder of what we're headed towards. "You should turn the light off. In case we need it later."

She blinks a few times, as if remembering herself suddenly.

"Yeah… good idea."

She clicks the flashlight off, plunging us into shadow. The lightning still reaches us a little, flashing through the gaps in the shed. The rain is *hammering* now. I can hear full streams of it running off the roof and splashing into the mud just on the other side of the shed wall. I imagine the storm getting even worse somehow, washing away the dirt, the shed coming loose from the ground, the rain carrying us down the mountain like an enclosed raft.

"You said you were running away from home?" I ask, hoping to make conversation, hoping to think of something besides our impending murders. "What for?"

Kylie doesn't answer me right away. For a moment I worry she might ignore me. For all I know, maybe she'd rather think about death than her home life.

"Getting away from my dad, mostly," she says. I'm relieved when she replies.

"Ah. He's an asshole, I'm guessing?"

"Mmm," Kylie says. "It wasn't just him, though. It was… everything, I guess. A lot of good it did me."

You poor girl, I think, and promptly catch myself thinking it. I feel sorry for her, but I'm also wholly aware of what I'm doing, what I'm projecting on her, *who* I'm projecting on her.

"Where were you planning to go?"

"To my sister's. Well… maybe. I didn't really know where I was going. I had this idea in my head, that I'd show up at my sister's place and she'd just let me crash there. But that's probably not what would have actually happened. We barely even talk. I don't think she would have been happy to see me. I just couldn't stay with him anymore." She sighs. "My dad, I mean…"

"And your mom?"

Lightning strobes against the shed again, this time incredibly bright, incredibly close, so that for an instant I see her on the other side of the shed, pulling her legs tighter against her chest, her face sort of *twisted up* in thought. The lightning must have been especially close, because as soon as it's gone, the thunder follows—a startling applause, stiffening me against the wall at my back.

"I have no idea where my mom is," she answers. "I guess she couldn't stand my dad, either."

And so she left you alone with him, I think bitterly.

I admit that I'm making assumptions, telling myself a story in my head which may or may not reflect the truth at all.

"Did you really speak to your husband?" Kylie asks suddenly. "You said he was sending help. Is that true?"

I falter, wondering if I should lie to her or tell the whole truth.

"I don't know," I answer honestly. "She had my phone and it started ringing. It was my husband. I managed to answer the call, but she destroyed my phone before I could say too much. I did scream, though. I told him I needed help. If he was on the other end, he heard me." Then, choosing optimism for both our sake, "I'm confident he heard me. He knows I'm in trouble."

God, I hope I'm right. I hope he called the police. I hope they're already on their way. If they can ping my phone's last known location, then maybe… maybe…

"Why were you staying at that woman's place anyway?" Kylie asks next. "You were there all by yourself?"

Well, because I was struggling. I needed *time off*. I needed *time away*. I needed *time alone*. These are the reasons I've given myself, but I see them now for what they are: excuses. In the dark, I touch the wedding band around my finger. I twist it back and forth, slick with my own sweat.

"I think I was running away, too," I say. Then, after a brief pause, "No, that's exactly what I was doing. I was running away."

"Running away from what?"

I'm smart enough to know this strange girl doesn't really care about me or my life. I would never expect her to. She's distracting herself, and perhaps distracting me from asking her anything more about her personal life, which is great considering that was my goal starting this whole conversation in the first place—to distract her. I'm more than happy to indulge, to fill the silence with something besides the storm and our own tumultuous thoughts.

"I had a daughter about your age," I say. "She died three years ago."

The change of tone in Kylie's voice is immediately apparent, as her interest is piqued. "How did she die?"

"It was a car accident. A bad one. She was killed alongside three of her friends."

"Wow," Kylie says, reflecting. "I'm sorry. That sucks."

I'm almost brought to laughter by her words. I manage to hold back, but I *do* smile, even under the circumstances. Something about those two words just strikes me as incredibly funny. *That sucks.* Such an understatement. Especially for something so tragic.

"Yeah," I say, still smiling. "It does suck."

"What was her name?"

Now the smile slips. I'm not sure why. It's not like I don't think about her constantly, her name always floating in the undercurrents of my thoughts. I can daydream and reminisce about her all day long, every day of the week, and yet somehow her name is so painful. As I falter, hesitant to answer Kylie's innocent question, suddenly it's cemented in my mind—*oh yeah, I've been running for a long time, haven't I...*

"Ivy."

Thank God it's pitch black in the shed, because I'd rather not show Kylie the tears that spill out of my eyes in two seconds flat upon speaking my daughter's name.

"Her name was Ivy."

We're interrupted by another violent lightning strike, close and brighter than daylight. In those flickering seconds, Kylie seems to notice something. I sit and listen as she crawls across the shed, toward the rear.

"Hey," she says.

"Yeah?"

The flashlight clicks on again. Kylie's on her knees, hunched over and studying the rear wall near the floor, or rather one board in particular.

"This board is coming loose," she says. "It's like... curling inward."

She's right. The bottom plank along the back wall appears to jut out from the rest on its righthand side.

"Hold this," Kylie says, and hands me the little flashlight.

I aim the light on the board in question, as Kylie tries to grab hold of its edge with her fingertips, tries to pull it further inward. To my amazement—and my ever-pounding heart—it bends with visible ease in her grasp. Lightning flashes again outside. Its light reaches brilliantly through the gap behind the loose board, which is what Kylie must have first noticed. She continues pulling on it, bending it, letting it go as her fingers slip, pulling on it again.

"It's kinda soft," she says.

I get even closer, crouching over her, shining the light downward.

"It's probably rotted over the years," I say. "From all the moisture."

Kylie manages to get her fingers *behind* the board, she's bent it so much, and from there she's able to pull, pull, pull until we both hear the wood softly cracking, breaking. The board crunches in Kylie's grasp so suddenly, she recoils against me, a long section of broken wood held in her hands.

"Oh shit," she says.

There's now a permanent opening in the bottom right of the shed wall, where the board broke off. Perhaps a little more than a foot in length.

"We might be able to squeeze through that," Kylie says.

I can already tell just by looking at it, there's no way I'm fitting through there.

"You might fit," I say. "I'm pretty sure I won't. But that's okay…"

"Maybe I can break it some more," she says.

Kylie hooks her fingers over the splintered, broken edge of the board and pulls. It doesn't bend nearly as much as the first portion had. The remaining board must be sturdier, nailed to another vertical one on the other side, without enough loose length left to pry it away with our bare hands. Kylie pulls and pulls, scraping the inside of her fingers against the broken splinters. I'm doubtful she can break any more off. She stops for a moment, out of breath.

"It's nailed pretty good, huh?" I say.

"I still think I can get it," she says. "I think I can pull it loose. Just... gimme a second."

"Kylie," I say. I eye the hole in the wall, the cool, rainy air pluming against us through its small opening. "If you can fit through that... you should go. You should run and get help."

"Let me try some more, at least," she says. "Hold on..."

"Kylie."

"I can't just *run and get help*," she snaps.

I can hardly see her in the shadows before me, but her voice alone paints a clear, heated picture of what her face must look like right now, all the same.

"I already tried once and look where that got me. I have no idea where I'm going, or where help might be. I'd really rather not go by myself. Just... hold your fuckin' horses and let me try this some more. Okay?"

Her voice is quavering. I remember the terror in her eyes earlier.

"Okay," I say.

I continue holding the light for her while she pulls at the

broken board. From what I can see, it doesn't budge. It doesn't bend. It doesn't pull away from the intact board above it one bit. This old shack is well built and sturdy. We're lucky there was a rotted portion to break at all. Kylie's fingers are literally bleeding. I want to tell her to give up before she hurts herself more than she already has, but I don't want to upset her. Soon she wears herself out. She stands up, hands on her hips, and paces across the shed. She kicks the door again for good measure. The reliable padlock on the other side rattles in reply.

"He built this place to keep people inside," I say.

"There has to be a way out," Kylie says, pacing nervously. "This thing's gotta be so old. It's rotting in *one* place, maybe it's rotting in others…"

"There *is* a way out," I say. I shine the flashlight on the opening again. "You can probably squeeze through there."

"But you can't."

"That's okay. Only one of us needs to get help. I'll be okay, I promise…"

"You're sure you can't fit through there?" she says. "You're not any bigger than me…"

"Well, that's not true."

I shine the flashlight over myself, namely my breasts, to which Kylie makes a sound—something between a scoff and a laugh. She can't help it because it *is* pretty funny, even if *nothing else about this situation* is.

"I've also got wider shoulders than you do," I go on. "There's no way I can fit through there."

"Okay, but maybe you should try it first, before you just give up on the idea."

"All right," I say.

Fine, I think.

I hand her back the flashlight. I lay on my back, craning my head as I reach one arm through the hole, into the cool storm outside.

"If I get stuck, it's your fault," I say.

She says nothing as I press my feet against the shed floor, scooting myself against the opening as I pull myself with my arm along the exterior wall. I push my head mostly through—blinking into the dark woods outside as rain pelts my face—and that's about as far as I get before my other shoulder meets the shed's interior. There's no way I'll fit. I'm too broad. Even if I was narrower in the shoulders, I'm certain my boobs would be the next obstacle.

Gritting my teeth, I pull myself back inside, my hair now wet and muddy for my efforts.

"There," I say. "I tried. I really did."

Kylie hesitates, shining the flashlight on me, then on the hole.

"I don't even know if I can fit through there," she says.

"I think you can," I say.

I know you can.

She's narrower in the shoulders. She's flat-chested. She's just all around smaller than me.

"The fact there was a rotting plank *at all* is a miracle. That you were able to make an opening is a miracle. For you. Maybe for the both of us."

"Fuck," she says.

"The sooner you get out of here… and the sooner you get help…"

"Yeah, yeah, yeah," she says. "No pressure or anything…"

She shines the light on me again. I smile to the best of my abilities.

"You can do it. You've made it this far."

"What if they get the jump on me again? That's what he did before. His headlights were off and I didn't see him coming until it was too late."

"They've got their hands full, cleaning up. If they come back anytime soon, it won't be with their headlights off. They aren't expecting either of us to have escaped, after all."

Kylie is silent. Reluctant. Pondering.

"Wait a second," she says. "What if I find a big rock or something… maybe I can break the lock from the outside."

"Kylie…"

"It's worth a try, isn't it?"

She's desperate not to do this alone anymore. I can't blame her. It's scary enough as it is. Like we've already established, however, this shack was originally built to keep people inside. Although I haven't gotten a good look at the padlock itself, I'm doubtful it's going to be flimsy enough to break with a rock.

"Sure," I say. "Take a look. But remember… we have limited time."

"Yeah, I know."

I trade places with her. She tries to hand me the flash-light again.

"You keep it," I say. "You might need it."

I tell her this, because I'm doubtful that I'll be leaving this shed anytime soon.

Kylie lies on her back like I did. She reaches through, pulls herself little by little. I watch with mild envy as her shoulders squeeze and shimmy out into the rain, and in another moment she's wiggled out entirely.

THIRTY-SEVEN

KYLIE

Kʏʟɪᴇ's not outside the shed thirty seconds before the rain has drenched her. She stumbles barefoot in the mud, searching for a rock. It's harder than she predicted. Eventually she wanders to the front of the shed to study the padlock in question and is instantly disheartened by what she finds. Not only is the padlock not rusted at all after all these apparent years, but the latch that's bolted into the shed door is nearly as formidable as the padlock itself. Thick steel. No wonder her kicks to the door did nothing.

Gotta find a big rock, she thinks.

Even in the back of her mind, she knows she's fighting a losing battle. She knows she's being a coward. She doesn't want to trek down the mountain alone. The thought of running into them again, being chased through the dark trees, hardly knowing where she's headed—she is utterly terrified.

Down in the man's basement, she'd behaved recklessly, desperately—*anything to escape.* Having actually escaped, however, followed by being caught all over again, her hope has been squashed, her despair renewed, that reckless desperation all but bled out of her. They're in the middle of nowhere. Who knows how many miles she'll need to run before she finds help? Perhaps the elements will kill her before those psychopaths ever do.

Farther along the dirt path that leads away from the shed—the dirt path she knows she should be racing down right now, instead of wasting time—she finds what looks to be a suitable rock. Chunky, heavy, fits well between both hands. She takes it back to the shed. With rainwater streaming down her face, down her back, she strikes the padlock with the rock several times. She also manages to miss a couple times, striking the lock with the edge of her hand instead. She ignores the pain, keeps trying. The padlock is unfazed. She tries bludgeoning the latch itself, which proves just as fruitless, as it's bolted firmly against the shed.

"Any luck?" Barbara shouts from inside.

Kylie wants to cry.

"No," she answers.

"That's okay. I'll be all right, Kylie, I promise. You've got to get down the mountain. Just follow the dirt road. If you see someone coming, hide in the trees until they pass, unless you're certain it's not one of them. Okay?"

Follow the muddy dirt road. Follow the muddy dirt road.

At least Dorothy had Toto, Kylie thinks. She chews the inside of her lip, keeping her emotions at bay.

"Okay."

"You'll be fine," Barbara says.

Kylie turns to face the dirt path that winds into the trees, out of sight. She's not sure what else to say, or if she should say anything, so she simply starts walking. She drops the rock along the side of the road. Her bare feet squelch in the mud. With each step between her and the shed, she finds a little more resolve, a little more courage, a little more *hope*. Maybe this will be different. Maybe she'll get away this time. Get away *for real*. She repeats Barbara's reassurances, which begin to sound more like common sense to her now.

They've got their hands full, cleaning up.

If they come back anytime soon, it won't be with their head lights off.

They aren't expecting either of us to have escaped, after all.

Kylie also reminds herself that it took them a good deal of time to arrive at the shack after leaving the lake. However, covering that distance on foot will take even longer. Just thinking about it drops a pit of dread in her gut.

But she has nowhere else to go but down.

Now and again she looks over her shoulder to see the shed growing smaller in the distance, until soon she can't see it at all through the rain and mist and gloom. The slope of the road steadily grows steeper. She walks partially into the weeds, as the road becomes increasingly wet, muddy, slippery. She shivers as the cold rain seeps into her bones.

In an effort not to think too much about the arduous journey ahead, she distracts herself with other thoughts, such as: *What will my life be like should I survive this? What will my dad think? Will he even care? Will he have a change of heart, or will he have fear struck into it at the mere notion of almost losing me, his baby girl?*

Kylie doesn't think so, but it's nice to imagine.

Through the shimmer of rain, she sees headlights.

She stops so quickly she nearly slips on her ass. She darts into the trees. She nearly slips again, nearly goes tumbling as there's a sharp, steep hill just off the side of the road she hadn't even noticed until now, it's so dark. She catches herself, pushes herself upright once more. She creeps down the slope a bit and waits.

Farther down the road, the headlights steadily swell, strobing as they pass behind the trees, weaving and winding. Then they're coming straight toward her. Kylie hunkers down. She pokes her head up, watches as the car comes closer, closer, its tires flipping mud, windshield wipers on MAX.

It's her car again. *Cassidy's.*

He'd told them the truth: that he'd be back before they know it.

The car goes by, struggling up the gradual slope in the wet mud. Kylie sits patiently, watches as its red taillights vanish into the mist.

THIRTY-EIGHT

BARBARA

My final words to her hang poisonously in the air: *You'll be fine.*

I listen intently, but she says nothing after that. She's just gone. She vanishes into the rain and thunder and now I'm left in this shed alone, crossing my fingers she makes it. I'm tempted to try the hole again. Maybe I *can* squeeze myself through with enough pushing, enough pulling, a little dislocated shoulder here, a little skin off my boobs there.

I'm not a religious person—I never have been, don't even know if I'm a believer of anything, truthfully—but I pray she makes it. I pray she gets down the mountain, finds an honest-to-God *paved* road, and flags down the first car she sees that isn't Cassidy's. I pray she gets help, saves herself... and maybe even saves me. I'm not sure about the last part, though. That's a lot to ask in this situation. It'll be hours before she gets in touch with the authorities, even longer before they make their way here and find me. Will it be too late then? Will Sterling have already come back to finish me off?

I remind myself that Hank might have already sent help my way. It's been a considerable amount of time since then. A couple hours, maybe? Maybe more? I'm not sure. Perhaps there are police already parked outside Cassidy's lake house looking for me, investigating, questioning. Cassidy won't be getting any sleep tonight, that's for sure. What a fool she is...

I decide to try pulling at the broken board at the rear of the shed some more. There's no doubt in my mind that Kylie's stronger than I am, and if the board were able to be pried out, she'd have done it. But I try nonetheless, with similar results. The board is secure.

I feel another hot flash coming on, even amid the storm's cool, moist breath coming through the hole. I take a seat next to it, lean back, my head against the shed wall, my cheeks simultaneously burning up and enjoying the cool air.

A sudden bright light beams against the other side of the shed, shining through the thin gaps around the door.

Headlights.

Shit.

He's come back already. Back to finish what he started. He'll probably kill me when he discovers Kylie isn't here. Then he'll be hunting her all the way back down the mountain. Unless he's already got her—caught her on his way up, got the jump on her again just like she feared, just like I told her *wouldn't* happen again.

You'll be fine.

The headlights grow their brightest as the vehicle comes to a stop right outside the shed door. My heart is racing. Do I sit where I am? Do I simply wait for what's coming? Or do I hide beside the door and hope to ambush him as he enters, catching him off guard and most likely ensuring my own demise by his retaliation?

The car door slams shut outside. I'm amazed I can hear it even over the rain drumming on the roof. The sound snaps me upright and onto my feet. I panic a little. I go to the door, lean my ear against it. Footsteps clap the mud outside on their way toward the shed. I withdraw slightly away from the door. The footsteps stop just on the other side. They take up the padlock, then release it, letting it thump. I step back, expecting the door to open, but it doesn't.

My visitor speaks, and it isn't Sterling after all.

"*Barbara?*" Cassidy calls through the door.

I'm stunned, to say the least. I distinctly remember Sterling *not* telling her where he was taking us. If she's here, does that mean he changed his mind? If she's alone, I highly doubt it. And she sounds very much alone.

"*Barbara, are you in there?*"

If she's come against her father's wishes, or perhaps even without him knowing, then she doesn't know whether or not anyone's inside. She's here on a hunch.

I say nothing in reply.

"*I know you're in there. This is the only other place daddy could bring you on such short notice…*"

Say she *does* know. She still doesn't know whether or not we're alive.

"Barbara? If you're in there… I want to help you."

Bullshit. It's the most bullshittiest thing I've heard in my entire life. Only someone as dense as Cassidy could believe that anyone else would be dense enough to believe it. She's obviously disobeying her father. Seeing as she's worried enough to make the trip up here, I'd also wager she's not just here to find out whether we're alive or not, but to make sure it's the latter.

"Are you…" Cassidy trails off. I lean closer, struggling to hear her over the storm. A deep growl of thunder in the distance. *"Yeah? Hello? Yeah, I'm… What is it?"*

She's on the phone. At this hour, I assume with Sterling.

"They're already at the house? Are you sure? Okay… yes, I know, I'm…" She pauses for a time. *"I did what you told me. Of course. I'm… I'm driving right now."*

With perfect timing, the sky lets loose another startling thunderclap.

"I'm driving, daddy. I did. I'm… Yes, that was thunder. I'm not outside. Well… no, I'm not outside. I'm doing exactly like you told me. Yes. I'm not lying…"

I hear a sound through the door. It's Cassidy's voice, I think. A choking sound. No, not a choking sound. She's become emotional, crying into her phone.

"Okay, yeah, I'm outside," she says. Her voice has gone ugly with tears. *"This whole thing's such a mess, daddy… They're gonna find out what I did. They are. I know they are. They are, daddy, and then they're gonna find 'em here and every-thing's gonna be over. Yes they will. It's a mistake to just leave 'em here like this. No. No, I…"*

She goes quiet again. Obviously Sterling is filling the

other end of the line with his argument. I can imagine the utter frustration in his voice, having some semblance of a plan and watching his daughter unravel it in real time.

"Listen, daddy, I'm sorry, but… but I have to go. I have to go. Okay? I'm sorry. I'm hanging up now."

Cassidy goes quiet. A dribble of hitching sobs escape her, as I assume she tucks her phone back into her pocket. The padlock scrapes the door again as she seems to fiddle with it. She lets it go again. Her footsteps slap away, back toward her car, its headlights still blazing through the gaps in the shed door. I focus on the light at my feet, still listening with my ear nearly pressed to the wood. The light is briefly interrupted as Cassidy makes her way back, standing before the door again. She mutters something under her breath. I have to really focus to hear what she says.

"I swear to God, this better not ricochet back…"

A moment of silence. *Rainy* silence. It takes all of that moment for me to understand what I just heard, what Cassidy just muttered—long enough that I'm caught completely by surprise by the sudden gunshot on the other side of the door. I flinch back, retreating into the corner beside the doorway. Cassidy bothers with the padlock again, scraping it through the latch's loop and tossing it aside.

Then the door wobbles open.

"Barbara?" she says, peeking through the gap into the shed's darkness.

I press myself firmly into the corner, into the shadows, away from the blinding glow of the headlights as Cassidy opens the door a bit more, points her gun into the shed. She aims toward the bloody floorboards where she expects us to be. Still standing outside, all I can see of her are her hands, gripping the gun tight, slowly slipping into view inch by inch as she moves inside. Hesitant.

"What the hell…" She steps far enough inside that I see the profile of her face—her confusion, her alarm. Her eyes flicker from the middle of the floor to the back, where I know she sees the hole we've made. "Oh my God…"

Then her eyes visibly glance to the side. Toward me. She senses me here. She *sees* me, a shadow in the murk, a peripheral phantom. She starts to turn. The gun turns with her. My feet carry me ahead, moving of their own volition. I reach for her, one hand going for the gun, the other for anything else it can grip, shove, subdue. It all happens so quickly and yet so slowly. I collide against Cassidy. I stare into her bulging eyes, her parted lips drawn firm with a gasp that's yet to escape her. I push her back stumbling. My hand closes around hers, around the grip of the gun as she retracts her elbow, brings the gun between us. As her back meets the opposite wall of the shed, the gun goes off.

Muzzle flash. Gunshot. Lightning. Thunder.

I jolt with surprise, though I don't feel anything. Not at first.

My body must know better than I do, though, as I suddenly find myself letting go. My hands slip away from Cassidy. My feet stagger back. I expect another gunshot to follow, but it doesn't come. She appears as shocked as I feel. I look down at myself, and before I can even understand the wet drizzle of blood soaking through the belly of my shirt, I lose all the strength in my legs. I go down. I sit hard on my butt, one hand to my stomach, the other patting the floor uselessly to stabilize myself. Cassidy pushes away from the shed wall, standing in the doorway once more, a dark outline framed by the dazzle of headlights and sparkling rain at her back, her stance that of a trembling foal about to buckle at the knees.

Shit. That's it, then.

With shaky hands, Cassidy pushes wet strands of hair out of her face, traces them behind her ear, then frantically clamps both hands around the gun, like it might get away from her if she doesn't.

"I'm sorry, but you had this coming," she says, her voice as shaky as her hands, her legs. "Y-you have to know you had this coming, Barbara…"

I draw my gaze along her shape down to the dusty floor of the shed, where her shadow pools over me like a cold blanket. Another shadow appears there, spills into the light between Cassidy's legs. I look up again to see it. A second shape. It moves into the shed doorway. Cassidy doesn't know it's there. She can't hear it. Can't see it. The shape behind her raises its arms over its head, holding something between both hands.

Even over the droning rain and the purr of thunder I hear the impact of the rock on the back of Cassidy's head. A meaty thump. Cassidy crumples into the shadow at her feet, onto the floor.

Shoulders heaving, dripping with rain, Kylie doesn't skip a beat. She drops the rock, snatches up Cassidy's gun. She comes to me, but wavers as she sees the damage.

"Oh God. Barbara…"

"I know." I don't know what else to say, so I state the obvious. "She got me."

"Come on." She tucks Cassidy's gun into the back of her waistband. In the back of my mind I pray she doesn't hurt herself with that thing. Look what it did to *me*, after all. "Come on, Barbara. We're getting out of here. Okay? Come on…"

She crouches with me, puts an arm around me, under the crook of mine. I climb to my feet, and it's only then I start to feel it—the gunshot wound. My stomach aches. My whole side aches. A burning, bruised feeling. It feels more like I've been punched than shot. But it hurts. Kylie guides me to the shed doorway, over Cassidy's body. She won't stay out for long, I think. Unless the blow to her head was fatal…

"Come on," Kylie repeats. "The car's still running."

She assists me to the passenger door. She opens it. I climb inside, out of the rain. My stomach flares with pain as I take a seat. Cassidy's got the heater running, though, which feels heavenly after stepping out of the cold rain.

"Wait here a second," Kylie says.

She shuts the door. I lean back in my seat, my head against the headrest, and watch through the streams of rain down the windshield as Kylie returns to the shed, the headlights lighting her up like she's on stage. She stands in the open doorway for a moment. She seems to consider Cassidy. I lean forward, cringing at the pain, and watch as Cassidy's body stirs on the ground. She's awake. Or waking up. Kylie pulls the gun from her waistband, and suddenly I find myself wanting to scream, wanting to tell her to stop.

Part of me wants Kylie to finish her off.

I flinch in my seat as a gunshot pops. My heart leaps into my throat. Cassidy's still moving, however. She's moving *a lot*, in fact. Then Kylie steps over her, bends down. I can't tell what's happening. A moment later, Kylie steps out of the shed and hurries to the driver's side. She climbs behind the wheel, slams the door shut. The rain thrums against the roof of the car.

"What did you do?" I ask.

"I shot her in the leg."

Kylie places something into the cupholder compartment between our seats. *Two* somethings. The gun, and Cassidy's phone. Smart move, I think. I lean back against my head-rest. I take a deep, deep breath, hoping it'll ease the pain but it doesn't.

Then the phone in the cupholder starts to vibrate. It buzzes loudly, jittering in place. Kylie picks it up. She stares at the phone but doesn't attempt to answer it.

"Who is it?"

Kylie holds it toward my face so I can see. The caller ID literally reads: *Daddy.* I want to puke. Kylie simply ignores the call.

"Call the police," I say.

"I can't," Kylie says. "The phone's locked."

"There should be…" A sharp intake of breath as the burning pain in my side suddenly spikes with a stabbing one. "There should be an emergency button."

Kylie studies the phone. "Oh. You're right. I see it."

She puts the phone to her ear.

Inside the shed, Cassidy crawls across the threshold, into the rain. She stops there, looks up, squinting into the headlights.

"Hi, um…" Kylie falters. I assume she's actually managed to reach the police, and dispatch has asked her what her emergency is. "I've been kidnapped…"

Impulsively, I reach my hand out to Kylie, gesturing for her to hand over the phone. It's only as my hand is outstretched that I see it's covered in my own blood. Nevertheless, Kylie hands it to me. I put the phone to my ear.

"Hello?" I say.

"Hello?" It's a woman on the other end. *"There's been a kidnapping? Who am I speaking to?"*

"My name is Barbara Harding. I'm with a young woman, Kylie…" I pause, looking at Kylie expectantly.

"Grenko," she answers.

"I'm with Kylie Grenko, a young woman who's been kidnapped and held at a property at Little Reed Lake. She was taken by a man by the name of Sterling…" I pause again, realizing I don't know his last name. Would it be the same as Cassidy's? "…and his daughter, Cassidy Barker…"

"Barbara Harding?" the woman repeats back to me. *"We've received a call from your husband. We've already dispatched officers to Little Reed Lake. Where are you now? Are you someplace safe?"*

I eye Cassidy outside, still slumped awkwardly in the shed doorway.

"I'm in a vehicle," I answer. I try my best to think straight, to give the clearest details possible. "No… no, we're not safe. We managed to take one of their vehicles... Cassidy Barker's vehicle... and... I've been shot."

"You've been shot? Where have you been shot, ma'am?"

"In the stomach," I say. "We're in a vehicle now. We are no longer at Little Reed Lake. I think we might be close, though, but I'm not sure..."

"Are you able to get to safety, ma'am? Who's driving the vehicle?"

"Kylie. Kylie's driving. We... we..." I take yet another deep breath. "We're going to drive ourselves down the mountain. I'm not sure where we are. We're going to try and reach a main road, if we can."

"Ma'am, I'd like you to stay on the line with me, okay? We're going to dispatch more officers to Little Reed Lake, and in the meantime we're going to try and get a location on your phone. All right?"

"Okay," I say. My eyes fill with tears. "Okay."

While I keep the phone to my ear, Kylie pulls on her seatbelt. She reaches across me and pulls mine on, too. Then she puts the car in REVERSE, pulls us out, puts the car back into DRIVE, and begins taking us down the mountain, following the muddy dirt road.

THIRTY-NINE

BARBARA

THE DISPATCHER STAYS in my ear, asking how I'm doing, asking about my wound, about our progress down the mountain.

I watch Kylie beside me as much as I watch the road ahead. Her brows are permanently knitted together, her chest a never-ending series of shallow ups and downs, both hands white-knuckled to the steering wheel as she navigates us along a series of hairpin turns. She brakes off and on the whole way down, as carefully as she can so that we don't gain too much speed. Even I can feel the car slipping and sliding in the mud.

"You're doing good," I tell her, putting the phone down to my chest for a second as I say it so that the dispatcher doesn't think I'm giving her a very strange compliment.

Kylie appears too worried to speak. All her attention is on the road. If we can even call it a road. It's more like a dirty Slip 'n Slide at this point. On the lefthand side is a major drop-off. One wrong move and we could go sliding right over the edge, right down into the trees toward the next stretch of road below.

I put the phone back to my ear, only to hear the tail-end of the dispatcher's latest question.

"I'm sorry," I say. "I missed that."

"How are the roads? Would it be safer for you to pull over and wait for assistance?"

No, I don't think it would be. For starters, I overheard that last phone call between Cassidy and Sterling. If I had to guess, Sterling is probably on his way up here right now to try and stop his daughter from doing something stupid. I don't have the energy to explain all of this to the woman on the other end of my call, though.

"No, I don't think we can afford to stop," I say.

Kylie brings the car to a near standstill as she takes the next turn. Not only is the road slippery, but narrow as hell. Now and again I feel the car's tires spinning underneath us, before miraculously finding purchase and lurching forward again. My heart lurches likewise in my chest each time, as I fear the next sudden start will take us over the edge. The next switchback puts the steep slope on our righthand side. My side. I peer out my window with the phone still to my ear, gazing down into the rainy slope below.

"You still with me, Barbara?"

"Yeah, I'm here," I say.

I wince, a sharp intake of breath as the pain in my gut blooms. I've never been shot before. I never imagined it would feel anything quite like this. Every now and then I look down at myself and marvel at the blood.

Rather than observe my own life oozing out of me, or

the perilous drop out my window, I loll my head in the other direction, toward Kylie behind the wheel, doing my best to keep the phone to my ear as the woman on the other end continues keeping me company.

Kylie looks as fearful as ever, but there's also a certain determination hardened on her brow. For an instant, she reminds me of Ivy. Such a willful girl, even from such a young age. Parents are supposed to teach their children, mold them, but in so many ways I swear Ivy defied the careful control of my hand, choosing to shape herself in spite of me.

In a moment of softening lucidity, I lower the phone from my face and I ask, "Have you driven before?"

Kylie's eyes dart fleetingly in my direction, refusing to leave the road for long.

"I never got my license, if that's what you mean," she replies. Oddly, her words don't worry me one bit. Maybe it's the gunshot, or the lack of blood, but I feel beyond anxiety. Beyond fear. "But I've driven before." She *does* take her eyes off the road now, for just a second to check on me, as I'm melting into my seat beside her. "How are you doing?"

"I'm doing okay," I say. Even in my state, however, I hear the sleepiness in my voice. "Don't worry about me. Just focus on the road…"

A sudden thought crosses my mind: *Am I dying right now?*

"Oh shit," Kylie says.

I blink my eyes and observe the focused alarm behind Kylie's gaze. I trace it to the road ahead, where I see the cause. Another vehicle. A larger vehicle, climbing the road toward us.

"That's him," Kylie says. "That's him. That's his truck."

Its headlights beam up at us through the glittering rain. Kylie brakes to a stop—the car still slides for a moment in the mud, turning ever so slightly out of place. Then we're stopped, face to face with the truck just below us. Sterling's truck.

"What's happening, Barbara?" the dispatcher asks.

"He's here," I answer.

"What do I do?" Kylie says. "Where do I go?"

"There's nowhere to go but forward," I say.

Obviously that's not an option, but at the moment it *is* our only option. There's no way we can reverse up the incline in this mud. There's no going around him, either. He's blocking us entirely.

But he doesn't know it's us yet.

The phone in my hand gives a little electronic chirp. I lower it. I'm still on a call with the dispatcher, but a second call is trying to come through.

Daddy.

I ignore the call. I put the phone back to my ear.

"Barbara, can you hear me?"

"I'm still here," I say. "Sterling's here, too. He's blocking the road. We're stuck." I turn to Kylie. "He still thinks we're his daughter."

"For now," Kylie says.

Again, the phone chirps in my hand. I lower it, glimpse the screen. Sterling's trying to call Cassidy again. I ignore the call a second time.

"*What's happening now, Barbara?*" the woman on the phone asks.

Ahead of us, the driver side door opens. A figure emerges into the rain, stepping out into the mud.

"He's climbing out of the truck," I say.

FORTY

KYLIE

KYLIE WONDERS if there's an age limit for heart attacks. Can a seventeen-year-old girl have one? She certainly feels she's on the brink. There's so much adrenaline coursing through her body, she feels lightheaded with it. Floaty. Buzzing. Sick. Beside her, Barbara seems rather calm, all things considered, as the stain on her wet shirt steadily grows bloodier, her face sweatier, paler.

She's dying, Kylie thinks.

"What do I do?" she asks again.

Her captor stands just outside the truck, squinting toward them through the rain. He must sense something is wrong. Probably asking himself why his daughter is simply stopped, not answering her phone.

"He knows it's us," Kylie says.

"He doesn't know it's us," Barbara insists.

He closes the door to his truck. He moves around the hood, comes to stand in front of the right headlight where he stops again, using one hand to shield his eyes from the rain as he peers toward them.

"He might be able to see us," Kylie says.

"Not through the rain," Barbara says.

"He can tell there are two of us sitting in here."

Kylie grips the steering wheel in both hands so tightly she swears it's about to crumble between her fingers. She forces herself to relax. She removes one hand from the wheel, reaches for the gun in the cupholder instead. It's their only real protection.

Well, that and the two-ton steel wagon under the command of my right foot, Kylie reminds herself.

The man, Sterling, takes two steps toward them, then stops again. It seems senseless to stand out in the rain like he is, but obviously he can tell something is wrong. He's wary of them. With each passing moment his subconscious is probably shooting up another red flare, another warning, another question as to why his daughter hasn't stuck her head out yet and said something to him.

He takes another step toward them. Kylie squeezes the grip of the gun. Then he stops again. Takes a step back. At this distance, Kylie knows she couldn't reliably shoot him. Until a few minutes ago, she'd never fired a gun before.

Pressed against the brake pedal, her foot itches to slam the gas instead.

Sterling takes another step back, then another, then returns to his truck. He climbs inside, leaves the door standing open. A moment later he emerges again. He returns to the road, caught between each of their headlights, moving swiftly with little to no hesitation in his steps. He's got something in his possession now.

"He's got a gun," Barbara says.

It's at that moment Sterling raises it, aiming toward their windshield. Kylie doesn't think. She just *does.* She floors the gas, the engine revving, sends the car hurtling through the mud directly at their target. The windshield cracks as a bullet penetrates the glass. Then Sterling is gone. The truck looms, a collision of blinding headlights before the nastier, metallic collision soon follows. They crash against the grille of Sterling's truck. Their car continues to move following the impact, however, their rear end sliding out from behind them, off the edge of the road, where gravity pulls them over and down into the sloping weeds, jostling them in their uncontrollable descent. They rock hard against the waiting trees. The car spins on its wheels, thrown wildly, until they abruptly hit something else, something low that topples them, rolls them clean over, the world through the windshield spinning like clothes in the wash cycle. Everything is crunching metal and bits of glass and wet rain in Kylie's eyes, Barbara's pained moans in her ears. Then they hit another obstacle, another tree or rock or who gives a damn, and the car stops rolling, is pulled around on its rooftop, until finally they come to a sudden halt, each of them dangling upside-down against their seatbelts. It's a long, silent, bewildering moment as Kylie's senses reorient themselves, as her skull pounds with all the blood rushing to her head.

"Oh… *God*," she groans.

She squirms in place, falls right out of her seatbelt and

onto the roof beneath her head. She pushes herself over, every joint and muscle feeling swollen and out of place. She tries to blink the dizziness away. Barbara still hangs upside down beside her, the curtain of her dangling hair a tangled mess. Her eyes are shut. Dazed? Unconscious? Dead? Kylie can't tell.

"Barbara," she says. She hurts so much, she can hardly find her voice. "Barbara… are you…"

Barbara's dangling hands are empty. The phone is nowhere to be seen. Neither is the gun. Kylie peers upward, as if it might somehow still be lodged inside the cupholder. It's not.

"Barbara, are you all right…"

Through the patter of rain, Kylie hears a collection of snapping branches and mud-sucking footfalls as someone hastily makes their way down through the trees toward them. It has to be Sterling, Kylie knows.

"Barbara," she says again. She grabs one of her dangling arms and gives her a shake. "Barbara, are you—"

Kylie screams as she's grabbed around the ankle. She's dragged through the shattered window, into the mud. Sterling stoops over her. His hands scramble across her body. She beats at him, kicks at him. She wriggles out from under him, crawls away with fistfuls of mud and weeds. He falls on top of her, forces her down.

"You little whore…" He tries to pin her down but she flails her limbs out from his groping hands. *"What'd you do to my daughter, huh? What'd you do to my Cass…"*

Kylie flounders beneath him. She rolls onto her back so she can better fend him off, batting his hands off her, reaching for his face. She tries to claw for his eyes but he pushes her hands away, wrangles them down against the ground. His grip slides down her arms, traces her body to her shoulders, to her neck, where his strong hands find the same bruises they left before and begin to squeeze.

FORTY-ONE

BARBARA

I MUST HAVE LOST consciousness during the crash. One second I'm tumbling around under my seatbelt—it's *me* hitting the seatbelt, but I feel like I'm being punched in the shoulder and chest—and then suddenly I open my eyes and everything is still. Quiet. It feels like it's been this way for some time now. A minute. An hour. A few seconds. I don't know. My head is pounding, full of blood. I'm upside-down.

For a vague, brain-foggy moment, I wonder: *Is this what it was like for her? During the crash?*

Except my daughter didn't get to wake up like I have.

Also that was a long time ago. This is happening *now*. I'm here right *now*. And I'm not the only one.

Kylie? I want to say but can't quite find my voice.

I reach for my seatbelt connector. I push one hand to the car roof below me as I disconnect my seatbelt, hoping to keep myself from collapsing on my neck as it releases me. My seatbelt clicks undone. I immediately thump onto the roof, barely tucking my head in during the brief fall. I crumble onto my side. My gut lights up in pain, and all at once I remember that, too—I've been shot.

There's noise close by. Movement and voices. Kylie's voice. Sterling's voice. A struggle.

I reach for my door but its difficult to open upside-down. I pull the handle, release the door open, give it a weak shove, and attempt to crawl out of the car on my hands and knees. Pulling myself through, my left hand happens upon something tucked into the wet weeds. I recognize its shape. Cassidy's gun. I grab hold of it. I pick myself up, or try to, struggling to get my feet under me. My stomach quivers in a dull, throbbing kind of way, sends me staggering against the car where I catch myself, a hand across my blood-soaked shirt. The rain is still falling, tattooing the dark with its wet sheen and pitter-patter hum.

Kylie is nearby. I hear her. Sputtering.

Since I'm already leaning against the car, I use it to brace myself as I slowly trace around it toward their voices. Lightning flashes in the sky, streaks of light and shadow through the woods. I glimpse them in the flash. Sterling, anyway. I see the top of his salt-and-pepper head on the other side of the overturned car. I keep going, one hand on the car, the other on the gun. I have to pause momentarily as my vision blurs, my head *fizzing* and swimming with some intangible light. Dizzy. I steady myself. It fades away, the darkness and the rainy shimmer returning. Thunder rolls through the clouds. I keep moving.

I see them both now. Kylie's on her back in the grass, Sterling straddling her, his hands around her throat, crushing the life right out of her. She's still fighting. She's still alive. She gropes at his upper arms, his shoulders, trying to stop him with hopeless results. I push away from the car in my approach. I don't think Sterling even knows I'm here, coming up behind them. Probably can't hear me over the storm. I hold my breath as a wave of pain spreads from my stomach through my hips, my groin. I think I really might be dying.

No. Not yet. Not before…

I arrive at Sterling's hunched back. I raise the gun, press the mouth of its barrel against the back of his head.

FORTY-TWO

KYLIE

KYLIE FEELS HERSELF FADING AWAY, the life slipping out of her body as her ears drum with blood and strange thoughts.

What a nightmare, she thinks.

To have made it this far, to have endured this much, only for him to win in the end regardless. She hates that his disgusting, monstrous face will be the last thing she ever sees, that her final moment will be here, looking up into his bared teeth, the rain dripping off the tip of his wrinkled nose. She continues batting at him with her pathetic hands. She can't even hold a fist anymore. Her arms fall limp against his, dribbling down them like the rain. Her mind wanders ever closer toward the cliff of unconsciousness...

That's when the gunshot startles her back from its edge.

Through the cold sprinkle of rain, her face is sprayed with sudden warmth. Fresh, sticky warmth. The muscular hands around her throat soften. The man on top of her bonks his forehead against her chin as he slumps forward. With her throat released, lucidity floods her. Her vision brightens, overcompensates, so that for a moment it's like she can see in the dark, the surrounding trees lit up with lightning that won't end. Then everything darkens once more. She can breathe. Her skull releases its pressure. She blinks her eyes but can't rid them of the red blotches caught in her eyelashes.

She fights to shove Sterling's body off herself. His head lolls against her. She shoves him over onto the ground, onto his back, and glimpses the horrid exit wound between his eyes—the very wound she's been spattered with.

Someone collapses at her feet.

Kylie sits up, finds Barbara in the mud, Cassidy's gun held loosely in her hand. She crawls for her, hovers. She peers up the slope they tumbled down, can see the wide grooves the car made in the earth in its violent descent. On the road above them, Sterling's truck is still parked, head-lights shining.

"Barbara." She shakes her by the shoulder. "Barbara? You okay?"

Obviously she's not okay. She's not responding. She's pale as a ghost in the wet dark. However, her eyes are slit-ted, blinking slowly. She's not dead yet. Still hanging on, for now. They're closer now to the next stretch of road below than the one they came from. Kylie doubts Barbara's ability to stand, or her own ability to drag Barbara up the slope to Sterling's truck.

"Barbara, hold on, okay? I'll be back. I'll be *right back.*"

Kylie hurries as fast as she can, bare feet squishing in the mud. She scrambles up the slope from whence they came, crawls through the fresh divots and trenches they made in their accident. Lightning douses the woods in harsh white. She keeps climbing, slipping, grabbing fistfuls of mud and weeds, blinking Sterling's brain matter from her eyes. She shudders—from the cold and squeamishness alike.

Hold on, Barbara. Just hold on a little longer. Please.

She reaches the road on shaky legs, shaky arms, out of breath. The truck is still idling, a ghost of exhaust in the rain. She reaches greedily for the door, pulls it open, hauls her trembling self behind the wheel. She shuts the door and the cab fills with her tired panting, the muffled rain. Peering distractedly into the rearview mirror, she spots herself there, a pink bloody residue down her face where the rain hasn't yet washed her clean. Oh well. No time for vanity.

The truck is an automatic.

"Thank God."

She has to sit forward, too short to sit comfortably where Sterling's got the seat positioned, too panicked to spend any time figuring out how to adjust it. She puts the truck into REVERSE. She peers into the rearview again, lets off the brake just a little, letting the truck roll back. She rolls steadily down, down, down toward the next hairpin turn, where she hopes to have enough room that she can swing back and put the truck into DRIVE the rest of the way down. Down to Barbara.

Please hold on.

She brakes as she nears the turn. She cranks the wheel, angles the truck gradually toward the next downhill stretch. She's done it, with room to spare. She shifts into DRIVE. She eases the truck ahead, its larger tires a little more capable in the mud than Cassidy's had been. She follows the road down a ways until she sees those upside-down headlights shining through the trees, signaling the crash. She comes to a stop, parks the truck, climbs back out into the rain. She trudges into the trees. Barbara's still lying just where she left her.

"Barbara? Are you still with me?"

FORTY-THREE

BARBARA

I DON'T THINK I've ever felt this cold in my life. I must be close to the end. Every raindrop is a stinging needle of ice upon my face, and yet I feel simultaneously numb all over. Even my stomach, which previously felt on fire, has turned cold inside me, my organs replaced with hunks of ice, chilling me to the bone. Yet I'm not even shivering.

Kylie came to me. After I saved her. After I blew a hole through the back of Sterling's head. As soon as I pulled the trigger, it was like all the strength I had gone out of me, like I'd been shot. Again, I mean. I collapsed into a useless pile of clothes and bleeding meat.

I blink my eyes and see the woods, see the rain, the odd flash of storm light. I listen as Kylie stands over me, tells me she's coming right back.

Then she's gone forever.

Maybe it's not forever, but it *feels* like forever. She scampers away into the rain, and I lay here for ages. My mind wanders to strange places—like when you're on the verge of sleep and your thoughts become silly, incoherent, like little pre-dreams before you actually fall under.

I begin thinking of Hank. Of how we met. Maybe it's that I'm currently dying that makes me think of it—how I first met Hank at his own mother's funeral. I know, not really the place to be making sparks, but to be fair it didn't happen as fast as that. I was merely friends with Hank's sister at the time, whom I'd met in college. Hank had lived two states away on some kind of work contract, but obviously came home when he'd received news of their mother's accident. She'd fallen, hit her head, had grown sleepy, took a nap, never woke up.

Life is so goddamn fragile, I can't stand it.

Anyway, as I'm lying in the woods with my literal life leaking out of me, I'm thinking of Hank, I'm thinking of him at his mother's funeral, seeing just what a wreck he'd been. He delivered the final eulogy. I still remember that eulogy. I remember the exact words his voice cracked on, when he fell apart so unapologetically. I know there exist many women in the world who are repulsed by the sight of an emotional man—an incredibly disturbing outlook in my opinion, if I may be so blunt—but I've always found myself on the complete opposite end of that spectrum. And maybe that's disturbing, too, in its own way. Maybe it says something about me, that I immediately fell head over heels for Hank simply by the way he fell apart delivering his mother's eulogy. There was a man so full of emotion, so unashamed of that emotion, to bear his soul to a room full of loved ones and strangers alike. Not only did that vulnerability speak volumes to his character, in my mind, but it spoke volumes to his love for the woman who raised him, the woman who played such an integral role in molding the man he grew to be—the man I soon fell in love with.

I only saw Hank fall to pieces like that one other time—the day of our daughter's accident.

I realize now I'm thinking of these things not because I'm terrified of my own death, but because I hate the thought of what happens after. What happens to those I love when I'm gone. To Hank. We both unraveled when Ivy passed, but we were right there together to help pick up each other's pieces again. If Hank has to go through it all over again, *without* me, *because* of me…

Am I losing you?

It's more than I can take, I think.

There's a voice in my ear. A girl's voice. A young woman's voice. It's her again. *Kylie.* She's begging me to wake up. She's begging me to stand. I don't know that I can. I can hardly move. I can't even wiggle my tongue or lips to form the words to tell her that. But apparently I don't need to. She takes me up by the arms and starts dragging me through the mud, through the trees. She drags me into a bright beam of light, then beyond it. An idling engine. She drops me for a moment. A door opens. A vehicle door.

"Come on, Barbara," she says, crouching over me again. "Barbara, I need you to get up. Help me, please."

I try. I really do. She lifts me under the arms again. I bend my legs at the knees, try to plant my feet in the wet mud, try to support myself as she hoists me onto the passenger seat of Sterling's truck. I hunch forward there, my hands on the dry seat. That's nice, I think. The dryness.

The warmth. I just need to crawl inside, get my legs in after me, out of the rain…

"Here we go…" Kylie says.

She grunts as she grabs me by the legs and lifts me the rest of the way into the vehicle, folding me awkwardly onto the front seat. It's all one seat, a cushioned bench from the passenger side to the driver's. I lay there on my side, my legs doing whatever they want under the glovebox, apparently. Kylie slams the door shut. It's incredibly warm in here, at least compared to the woods. The heater's blowing. The driver side door opens. Kylie climbs into the truck.

"Stay with me. We're almost there. Okay?"

Okay, I think but can't say.

I remember feeling like this one other time in my life— my first time getting stoned. I think I was nineteen. I couldn't get up from the couch. I couldn't even speak. I feel like that now, like I'm just stuck in one place. But I *am* awake. I'm still breathing. I'm still alive. I plan to stay that way, for as long as I can. I don't want to die. Not yet.

I want to see Hank again.

FORTY-FOUR

KYLIE

STERLING'S TRUCK is so much easier to maneuver through the slick mud than Cassidy's car, although Kylie still has to sit forward in the seat to see the road properly, to make sure they don't go spilling off another hillside.

It's not long before the road evens out, taking them through the trees toward an unknown destination. Kylie can't imagine they have much farther to go.

The worst of their dangers are behind them—Cassidy, Sterling, the treacherous switchbacks. Kylie's only immediate concern now is getting Barbara to rescue, before...

"We're almost there," she says aloud. "We're almost there..."

She says it not only for Barbara's sake, but her own as well.

I'm almost there. I'm almost there...

Under the repetitious squeal of the windshield wipers, the squeaky jostling of the truck's suspension, and the constant hum of rain on the roof, Barbara murmurs something. Kylie glances her way, lying across the seat with her neck craned, eyes wide and blinking in her direction. The look in Barbara's eyes is startling. A look of surprised recognition. Disbelief. Bafflement. Her mouth is open, and Kylie can see her tongue moving behind her teeth, trying to form words.

"Ivy..." She draws her gaze along Kylie's body behind the wheel. She reaches for her, a hand on Kylie's leg. She furrows her brow with a certain kind of hurt Kylie understands to be beyond the physical variety. *"Ivy..."*

Kylie isn't sure what to say, or if she should say anything. Obviously Barbara is delirious.

"I'm..." She stops herself. She focuses on the road. "We're almost there. Just hold on a little longer."

Just a little longer.

Truthfully, Kylie can't believe Barbara is still hanging on even now, even if only by a thread.

The truck rattles onward until the road comes to an abrupt end, butting up against another. Kylie is promptly faced with a decision. It's difficult to see each direction of the new road in the headlights, under the rain and in the dark, but from what Kylie can tell, one direction appears to be continuing *down* the mountain. She cranks the steering wheel hand over hand that way, follows the new road along a gradual downward slope.

She eyes the gas gauge, sees they have less than a quarter tank left. She prays they're going in the right direction, that she didn't just make the wrong turn, that in an hour from now she won't be out of gas, stuck in the middle of nowhere with no help in sight.

She didn't make the wrong turn. She sees something ahead.

Lights. Flashing lights.

Red and blue. Red and blue.

"Oh my God," she says aloud.

She presses on the gas. She's tempted to forego the road altogether, cut straight through the trees toward those beacons of hope, but chooses to stay the course instead, find the closest turnoff that will take her there. Her heart is beating fast again, this time for something *good*, something she wants, something that's so close she can almost taste it.

She passes a few turnoffs she doesn't suspect will lead her to the police lights, until finally she comes to one that feels right, branching off in their general direction. She takes it. The truck bobbles rather violently with the fervor of her steering, swinging them onto the new muddy path. The rain seems to have let up a little. Only a little. She cranks the wheel again, following the bend, then around another, and then the lights are straight ahead, within reach.

She pulls out from the trees, into a clearing, and realizes they're back. It's the same property as before, by the lake. Cassidy's place. There are three new vehicles parked out front, two of them police cruisers with their lights going. Kylie can hardly contain herself. She brakes to a stop, their lights soaking her in blue and red, blue and red, and suddenly Barbara is stirring, muttering something weakly under her breath.

"No," she says. She blinks her eyes up at the roof of the cab, squinting warily. "Oh, God, no…"

"It's okay," Kylie tells her. "We're here. We're here, Barbara!"

Kylie unbuckles herself. She throws open the door, jumps out into the rain again, bare feet almost slipping out from under her as she chases across the wet clearing to the uniformed officers, screaming for help.

FORTY-FIVE
BARBARA

When I see those lights flashing into the truck's cab, I think it's happening all over again. She's dead again. I'm back where it all started. Back where it all ended. One or the other or both. I've forgotten the difference over the years, between the start and the end. To be honest, I think I've found myself in a kind of *living purgatory*—not so much a place between death and the afterlife, but a state between living and… *not?* A meandering, mindless, static kind of living where nothing matters anymore because *nothing holds any meaning.* That's grief as a whole, in my experience. A living purgatory. When what once had incredible meaning is lost, everything that's left feels blunted, deadened. It makes sense, I suppose, that when I'm actually *truly* dying, I'm a little confused by the whole ordeal because I've already been living like the walking dead for three years now, so… *what is this?* Where am I? What's happening?

The passenger door opens. I'm swarmed by uniformed men. But instead of informing me that my daughter's been killed in a terrible rollover accident, they're carrying me in their arms, lugging me through the rain and placing me into the backseat of one of their cruisers, telling me the whole way that help is coming, help is close, they're going to take me closer, I just need to stay awake, stick around a while longer.

I'm so comforted by the thought of being saved that I can't help shutting my eyes against their wishes.

———

When I open them next, I'm transported. The woods and the dark and the rain are gone. My vision is instead confronted by *white*. So much white. Some intermittent beeping. I'm lying down, slightly propped up with my head on a soft but crinkly pillow. It's no longer cold, but it's not exactly warm, either. My head is bowling ball heavy, so that I can't lift it from the pillow. But I can move again. A little. I squeeze my hands into fists at my sides, just to prove to myself that I can.

"Barbara?"

A chair creaks. Footsteps sweep toward me. A figure appears, darkening the otherwise *bright white* of everything. His scent washes over me. Sweet and earthy.

"Oh…" he says, and his teeth wink at me, smiling. "My God, you're awake."

"Am I?" I say.

Hank snorts with amusement. I blink some more, until finally I see him properly, not through a sleepy haze. And what a sight for sore eyes he is. My heart swells as I take him in. The look on his face, the visible relief behind his gaze, is enough to fill my heart close to bursting.

"Yeah, you're awake," he says.

"Wow." I look down at myself. I feel something tight around my middle, across my stomach, which I figure must be the bandages they've wrapped me with. "I'm surprised…"

"So were the doctors," Hank says. "Which isn't the most reassuring news, let me tell you. They pulled a bullet out of you. Not to mention all your other cuts and bruises. You… well, you really went through hell, Barb."

Hank smiles again, but his eyes are still weighed down with that *sad relief,* the look of someone who's come so close to losing something dear to them. I want to kiss him.

"I want to kiss you," I tell him.

Seeing as I can't lift my head, he comes to me instead. I feel his warm, strong hands on either side of my face as he presses his lips to mine. I've always loved kissing him. A shame we've done it so sparingly these last few years. I decide right now, with his lips on mine, that we're going to do a lot more of it going forward. He pulls away from me, still holding my face, and peers into my eyes until that *sad relief* melts away, as it appears he finally accepts that I *am* awake, I *am* alive, that he doesn't need to worry so much now, and his brow softens, his gaze warms to mine.

Only now does my mind circle back.

"The girl," I blurt out. "Kylie…"

Hank looks confused, but only for a second. He nods.

"Oh yeah, she was here. They discharged her yesterday. You were still out, then."

"Wait, yesterday? How long has it been?"

"Just a couple days. She left with her dad."

Her dad, I think. I recall our brief conversation in Sterling's shed, wherein she'd told me she'd ran away from home to get away from him specifically. I suppose I don't know the details, what *exactly* she was running from, how typically rebellious she might have been. I know nothing about Kylie, really. Yet I immediately find myself worrying about her, wanting to know she's okay.

"I think she's okay," Hank says, perhaps seeing my concern. "All things considered, she made it out in much better shape than you."

"Yeah. I guess…"

"She stopped by to check on you, though. She wanted me to tell you thank you, when you woke up."

"Thank you?"

"For saving her life."

Hank takes hold of my face again and plants a big kiss on my forehead, then on my cheek.

"I'm so glad you're okay."

"What happened to Cassidy?"

I can still picture her writhing around inside that shed, after Kylie put a bullet in her leg.

"She was arrested," Hank says. "They've still got her. The police want to speak to you, too, of course. You know, to get your side of the story."

My side of the story. Where do I even begin? Obviously at the start, I know. It's just, at the tail-end of it all, everything seems so chaotic and senseless.

"I'm going to go let the doctor know you're awake,"

Hank says. "Okay? Hold tight."

As happy as I am to see Hank again, I'm grateful for the moment alone. The last few minutes, my mind has gradually filled up with the memories of everything, the tension of those near-death moments stirring up inside me like a shaken soda can. I take a deep breath. I remind myself that Sterling is either in a body bag or on a cold slab somewhere. Cassidy is behind bars. Kylie is—relatively—safe. *I'm* safe.

I'm safe.

My body doesn't seem to believe it yet. I'm still on edge, unsure how to ease the sensation. Probably something to do with the minor fact I'm still recovering from near-fatal wounds.

I'm alive. I'm safe.

When the doctor swings into my room with her clipboard, and my husband follows right behind her, flashing me his handsome smile to reassure me of these things, I finally begin to believe them.

I'm alive. I'm safe.

I grow hot under my hospital gown, my chest flushing with heat, my face burning red, beads of sweat prickling along my upper lip, my temples. I return my husband's smile. I take another deep breath, as the doctor asks me if I'm comfortable, apparently noticing the sweat I've broken into.

"Just a hot flash," I say.

My husband appears next to me, holding something. A folding fan, brought straight from home. He begins fanning me while I answer the doctor's questions, and suddenly everything starts to feel good again.

FORTY-SIX

KYLIE

"YOU SURE THAT'S EVERYTHING?" Kylie's sister asks with one hand on the hatch of her Subaru, a few boxes of Kylie's things in the back, including the backpack and tote bag she'd originally stuffed full of clothes the night she'd first tried to leave. The only thing the police weren't able to recover from that night was her phone.

"That's everything," Kylie says.

Georgia slams the hatch shut.

"Do you need to say goodbye to dad, or anything?"

"I already did."

It's true. Kylie told her father goodbye before Georgia even arrived to pick her up. She couldn't get him to stop watching TV for five seconds to acknowledge her eye to eye. Without turning his head, he'd simply said, "All right, I'll see you around, I guess."

Maybe saying goodbye is just too hard for him. Maybe he's afraid of all the emotions he'd feel.

As if, Kylie thinks.

No, the truth is that her father is bitter, hates the idea that she has someplace else to go, someone else she can lean on, that she isn't dependent on him and he can't control her anymore. When he'd shown up at the hospital to pick her up, he didn't ask her a single thing. Not even if she was all right, not anything. He'd simply strolled in, said "Let's go," and that was that.

Legally speaking, Kylie's not even sure she's even *allowed* to be moving out like this—she's not an adult yet—but it seems her father is done trying to stop her. Perhaps he doesn't want any scrutiny on him, either, after her harrowing story has already made it to the news outlets.

Kylie doesn't think she'll miss him at all. The feeling is probably mutual.

In fact, as she climbs into the passenger seat beside her sister, she feels overwhelmed with *lightness.* Relief. As well as a sudden rush of excitement, like she could jump back out and run laps around the car. She's seen dogs do that before. They call it *the zoomies.* She thinks she's experiencing that now. Human zoomies.

Instead of racing around like a maniac, however, she simply smiles to herself, and appreciates this new view of her childhood home growing smaller over her shoulder, the setting sun casting a warm glow over everything as her sister's car carries them both away.

Kylie's in the middle of unpacking her clothes, hanging them in her new bedroom closet, when there comes a knock on her bedroom door. The door is already open, but Georgia stands in the doorway, announcing herself.

"How's it going?" Georgia says.

Kylie shrugs, gesturing to the bags of clothes she's still sorting through.

"It's going."

She looks at her sister, as a stream of sentimentality bubbles up to the surface of her mind, things she'd wanted to say during their drive over but couldn't find the courage to do so. She decides to start with the easiest.

"Thanks again, by the way. For letting me stay here a while."

"No problem," Georgia says. "You can stay as long as you need."

Really? Kylie wants to ask, but doesn't because she doesn't want to sound clingy or desperate or anything of the sort. Part of her still suspects that her sister is only doing this out of some familial obligation, that she'd really rather Kylie not be here at all.

"Are you *sure* it's okay?" she blurts out. She's tired of this insecurity. Maybe if she confronts it head on, she can learn from it, or at the very least put it to rest. "Because if it's not, you know... I can totally find someplace else to—"

"Kylie, if it wasn't okay, you wouldn't be here right now in the middle of unpacking." Georgia steps fully into the room. She approaches Kylie with a look that reads *'what are you even talking about right now?'* which Kylie appreciates more than anything. She opens her arms, hugs Kylie around her shoulders. Kylie would hug her sister back, but her arms are still full of clothes. "I wish you'd called me sooner. I didn't realize you were having such a hard time, like I was."

Kylie could cry right now. It's everything she wanted to hear. It's everything she thought she was crazy to ever expect to hear. She holds back her tears, though. A little, anyway. When her sister pulls away from her, she quickly swipes under her eyes where a tear or two disobey orders. Georgia grimace-smiles at the sight of those tears.

"I mean it," she says. "I'm glad you're here. I'm excited."

She does a cute little shoulder shimmy as she says this, to emphasize how excited she is. Kylie can't help smiling back. It'll take a while longer for Georgia's truth to settle into her—years of feeling unwanted, of feeling like a burden, like trash nobody wants around but can't get rid of, won't be undone in a single night. But it's an incredible start.

"I'm excited, too."

Before either of them can say anything more, there comes *yet another* knock, from elsewhere in the house. The front door. Georgia looks over her shoulder, then back at Kylie with a furrowed brow.

"I'll go see who that is…"

As Georgia starts down the hallway, Kylie's first instinct is to imagine a slew of outrageous horror scenarios—that upon answering the door Georgia will scream, and suddenly that psycho woman will appear in the hallway, coming to finish what she and her now-deceased father started. Kylie has random thoughts like these all the time now. Not to mention the nightmares…

But instead of a scream, what she hears are voices. One of them Georgia's. After a brief moment, Georgia calls to her with a certain levity in her voice, like she's just finished laughing at something.

"Kylie," she calls. *"There's someone here to see you."*

Kylie hesitates. She takes an indecisive step toward her bedroom doorway, her arms still full of clothes. Finally she drops them to the floor and goes to see who it is.

She turns the corner in the hall, where she finds her sister standing in the front doorway. On the porch outside, illuminated by the single-bulb sconce by the door, a woman waits. The woman beams upon seeing Kylie. There's a certain, warm *neediness* in the woman's eyes, like she's been looking forward to this moment for a while now.

"Barbara," Kylie says, genuinely stunned to see her here. She joins her sister in the doorway. "What are you doing here?"

"Well, I was just in the neighborhood, and…" Barbara shrugs, fully aware of how phony this sounds. "I wanted to see you."

"You're welcome to come inside," Georgia says.

"Oh, that's all right," Barbara says. "I won't stay long. I just hoped I could speak to Kylie for a minute, is all. We could even talk out here. It's nice out tonight. Would that be all right, Kylie?"

Kylie hardly has to think about it.

"Yeah, of course," she says, and brushes past her sister, onto the porch. "I'll be in in a minute."

Kylie shuts the door behind her. The crickets are singing up a storm in the lawn, in the nearby dark. It's still plenty warm outside, even though the sun's gone down. The air clings to Kylie in an instant, like a fresh coat of sweat. She's used to it.

She looks Barbara in the eye, the hint of a smile on both their mouths.

The first words out of Kylie's are, "How did you know I was here?"

"Your sister," Barbara admits. "Don't be mad at her. I looked you up on Facebook and saw you hadn't been online in such a long time. But she was, so…" Barbara sighs deeply, clearly anxious. "Here I am."

"No, it's fine. It's *great*. I'm glad you're okay," Kylie says, and means it. "I mean, I knew you were okay and everything, but…"

But the last I saw you, you were unconscious in a hospital bed recovering from a gunshot to the stomach, and that was only a couple weeks ago.

"Thank you," Barbara says, "I'm a little surprised how well I healed up, all things considered…"

A silence begins to form, and both Kylie and Barbara start to speak in an effort to squash it. Kylie's more than happy to let Barbara take the reins, however.

"Anyway, I wanted to see you again, because, well…" In the warm porch light, Kylie sees Barbara's eyes glisten, moisture springing up from the wells of her words. "I wanted to say thank you. For saving my life that night…"

"Oh…" Kylie isn't so sure Barbara's account of that night is entirely accurate. "I mean, it was definitely a *mutual* saving, I think…"

"I just wanted to tell you that myself, face to face. For

everything. I'm sure you've heard this plenty these past couple weeks, but... you were very brave that night, Kylie. You *are* very brave. And I'm sure a lot of people have expressed how proud of you they are, for fighting like you did."

Kylie has not, in fact, heard this. She's heard *brave* a few times, yes, but not proud. Come to think of it... has she *ever* heard that before? *Proud?* Directed at herself? If she ever has, she truly can't remember it.

Barbara wipes the moisture from her eyes. There's a lot more meaning behind her words than the words themselves would suggest, Kylie knows. The emotion isn't for her alone. That *neediness* Kylie noticed before is still there, a wanting for something Kylie isn't entirely sure she can provide Barbara. But she can't say she's opposed to trying, either.

"I also wanted to ask you," Barbara goes on, "if you wouldn't mind getting lunch sometime? If that wouldn't be, you know, too *weird,* or anything. It would be my treat. And if that doesn't seem like something you'd be interested in, I completely understand, so don't feel like you have to—"

"Yeah," Kylie says. "I'd be down for that. Definitely."

Barbara looks stunned. "You would?"

Kylie has to try not to laugh. "Yeah, I'd like that. Any time. I'm even free this weekend. I just... well, I don't currently have a phone. My sister's taking me to get one tomorrow."

"Oh, that's fantastic," Barbara says. "I'll just... I'll message your sister my number, then. Then you can have it when you've got your phone. Would that work?"

"Yeah," Kylie says. "Sounds perfect."

Barbara looks so relieved, like all the tension and anticipation and *fear of rejection* she'd arrived with has evaporated from off her shoulders.

"Perfect," she repeats.

"And thank you too, by the way," Kylie adds. "You know. For saving my life that night. A couple times, at least, I'm pretty sure."

Barbara beams. "It was nothing."

They both laugh, but their laughter is soon followed by yet another stretch of silence. Even so, there's nothing awkward about it, Kylie thinks. It's rather comfortable.

"Well, it's getting late," Barbara says. "I'll let you get back to your evening. Hopefully I'll hear from you tomorrow? Or whenever."

"You'll be the first person I message when I get another phone in my hands," Kylie says.

"All right. Sounds good. Goodnight, Kylie."

"Goodnight, Barbara."

Barbara gives a brief wave as she turns and starts down the porch steps, down the sidewalk toward her car parked at the curb. It's the same car Kylie saw parked outside the lake house that night, which means Sterling must not have been able to get rid of it, like he'd planned. In retrospect, Kylie realizes their captors hadn't handled *anything* very well that night.

Up against a duo like me and Barbara, though, who would?

Kylie smiles privately as she watches Barbara climb into her car. Then she steps back inside and locks the door behind her. Her sister is waiting in the front room. She looks up from the sofa where she's scrolling on her phone, peering toward Kylie expectantly.

"Sorry, I should have told you," she says. "I hope that wasn't weird for you. I just thought—"

"No, it was good," Kylie says. "We're gonna get lunch this weekend."

"Oh, good!" Georgia exclaims, genuinely happy to hear this. "Yeah, I chatted with her online a little bit. She seems like a pretty cool lady."

"Yeah, she is," Kylie says. "Anyway, I'm gonna finish unpacking my stuff, and then probably get ready for bed."

"Okay," Georgia says, and offers Kylie an affectionate smirk.

Kylie returns to her room. She gathers up the clothes she dropped onto the floor, begins attaching them to hangers in the closet. She does this with a permanent smirk of her own glued to her face.

It's been a long time since she's had so much to look forward to.

EPILOGUE

THE ONLY THING sadder than crying in an empty cemetery is crying in a crowded one.

Luckily I'm not crying at all. Not today. Nor is the cemetery crowded. It's a Tuesday morning, it's mildly overcast, the sky a mixture of pale gray against some darker, wetter clots in the distance.

I'm sitting on the grass in front of my daughter's headstone.

I've sat here many times over the course of the last three years. And yes, I *have* cried here many times. Just not today. Today I'm feeling rather happy. Sublime, even. Maybe that's a stretch. I just don't think I've felt this good in so long that it's hard to measure.

I've come to my daughter's grave today in an attempt to share my happiness with her, or at least with the *idea* of her. Maybe she's listening, maybe she's not. If there is such a thing as an afterlife, I hope my daughter's got better things to do there than listen to her earthbound mother prattle on

about her new job, or her renewed love for her husband—
your father!— or the new friend she's made, a young woman
by the name of Kylie Grenko.

I've come to my daughter's grave today, on this oh-so-
happy day, because I want this place to be *that*. A happy
place. Not what it was. Not what it used to be. I used to just
come here to be sad. I mean, I was sad all the time, so it was
more like an extension of that sadness, or a doubling down,
if you will. I would come here to wrap myself in my grief
and soak in it until I was proper pickled with melancholy.

But my grief is changing now. Transforming. *Evolving.*
Did you know that grief is a living thing? It gestates. I've
carried it inside myself longer than I carried my own
daughter. I gave it everything I had, until I had almost
nothing left. It almost killed me. But now it's shifting, like I
said, preparing to be born into something new, something
better. Better for the both of us.

And I'm ready.

Our Beloved Daughter
Ivy Louise Harding
2004 - 2021

A SPECIAL THANKS

Dear brave reader,

I must say thank you. Without readers like you, authors like me wouldn't be allowed a paddle in this violent, ever-changing sea—otherwise known as the publishing world.

I only write these twisted, twisty stories with the utmost love and sincerity, so to be granted your curiosity means more than you can ever know.

If you have a moment, let me know your thoughts by leaving a review. It's a simple gesture that means the world to us indie publishers and helps other curious readers like yourself find books like mine. I'd greatly appreciate it.

Thanks again! There are plenty more thrills to come!

With love,
Beau